To David, Harry and Joe
with all my love

ORCHARD BOOKS

338 Euston Road, London NW1 3BH
Orchard Books Australia
Level 17/207 Kent Street, Sydney, NSW 2000

First published in 2011 by Orchard Books

A Paperback Original

ISBN 978 1 40830 428 0

Text © Keris Stainton 2011

The right of Keris Stainton to be identified as the author of this work
has been asserted by her in accordance with the Copyright, Designs and
Patents Act, 1988.

A CIP catalogue record for this book is available from the British Library.

1 3 5 7 9 10 8 6 4 2

Printed in Great Britain

Orchard Books is a division of Hachette Children's Books,
an Hachette UK company.

www.hachette.co.uk

JESSIE ♥ NYC

Keris Stainton

ORCHARD

Chapter One

"I can't believe we're going to New York," Jessie said.

"I know," Emma grinned. "Am I dreaming? Pinch me."

Jessie pinched Emma's arm.

"No," Emma said. "We're really going. To New York. For the summer."

"I know," Jessie said.

"That top looks great," Emma said, leaning back. "I'm glad you bought it. We have to make a good impression right from the start."

"On who?" Jessie asked, not for the first time.

"On New York!"

"I think you're overestimating New York's

interest in us," Jessie said, smiling.

"You never know. And you can't be too careful. Who knows, we might meet two boys at the airport."

"I think Taylor's put me off boys for life," Jessie said.

"Give over!" Emma said, squeezing her best friend's arm. "Yes, Taylor's an idiot and you're better off without him, but you just have to put that behind you. New York boys will be way hotter than Taylor, I promise you."

Boys or no boys, Jessie was thrilled with the outfit of J Brand jeans and a Marc Jacobs top that Emma had insisted she buy. She felt different. She was trying to think of herself as "New York Jess". New York Jess wouldn't have fallen for Taylor. New York Jess wouldn't be running away from her broken heart. But at least New York Jess had a fabulous pair of jeans. Every cloud has a silver lining.

As the flight attendant walked down the aisle, checking everyone had their seatbelts fastened, Jessie felt butterflies rise in her stomach. She'd been winding Emma up all day, but she couldn't believe they were getting to spend the summer in New York either. She'd been dreaming about it for so long and finally it was going to happen. And now it was going to be better than she'd imagined because Emma was going to be with her. She smiled at Emma, who was bouncing up and down in her seat with excitement. They were going to have an amazing time. And whatever happened, at least there was no risk of bumping into Taylor.

She still couldn't believe she'd been so stupid. She'd fallen for the oldest trick in the book. She'd liked Taylor Hutchinson for ages. She'd seen him the first day of her new school – after her parents had split up and she'd moved to Manchester with her mum. Taylor was so... God, it sounded ridiculous because she should have had more sense...but he was so dangerous-looking. Like he didn't care about anyone else, about what anyone thought. He was all floppy hair and brooding eyes, but she'd thought he was different inside because he'd been the first person to smile at her. She knew why now, of course – he just wanted to get into her pants – but at the time, her first day in a new school when she was feeling possibly more insecure than she ever had in her life before, he'd smiled. And she'd thought that underneath the hair and the glare he turned on the teacher as soon as he entered the room, he wasn't as bad as he wanted people to think. She really couldn't believe it. She'd thought he was good and sweet inside. But it turned out his insides were just as hard and mean as his outsides. Why did people say you couldn't judge a book by its cover? In Jessie's experience you totally could.

Emma grabbed Jessie's hand as the engine started to make that weird squealing noise. This was the part where Jessie realised how completely ridiculous flying was. They really expected this great, huge hunk of metal to just lift up into the sky? Apparently they did.

Emma fell asleep not long after take-off, but Jessie was too excited to sleep. Too excited and, if she was honest with herself, too nervous. She knew her mum had changed, she could hear it in her voice on the phone. She was all "New York". All parties and bars and weekends in the Hamptons. And, for all Jessie knew, all loved up with the director of her play. Actually she had no idea if anything was really going on between her mother and Jack, but she'd always suspected his interest was more than professional. He'd taken her mum and her play to Broadway; he couldn't have done that out of the goodness of his heart, could he?

And then there was Ben, who her mum and her mum's play had also taken to New York. Jessie hadn't really mentioned Ben to Emma. Not lately anyway. She'd tried not to even think about him, but here he was, popping into her head as her eyes stared, unfocussed, at some crappy Jennifer Aniston rom-com on the screen in the back of the seat in front. He'd stood in the rehearsal studio staring at Jessie in the mirror whilst reciting the lines for his leading role. And she'd stared back and felt her stomach do a little hiccup of excitement. If Emma was right and Jessie needed a new boy to help her get over Taylor, maybe Ben was the one.

"Ladies and gentlemen, as we start our descent, please ensure your seat backs and tray tables are in their full upright position. Make sure your seat belt is securely fastened and all carry-on luggage is stowed underneath the seat in front of you or in the overhead bins. Please turn off all electronic devices until we are safely parked at the gate. Thank you."

Jessie and Emma waited respectfully for the announcement to end before grabbing each other's hands and squealing.

"I can't believe we're about to land in NEW YORK!" Emma squeaked.

"Me neither," Jessie said. "Oh my God, Em!"

They stared at each other and then Emma, her face serious, said, "I know."

The flight attendant came to make sure they'd complied with the instructions.

Once she'd gone, Emma said, "Are you worried about seeing your mum?"

Emma knew how much it had hurt Jessie when Natalie had moved to New York, however much Jessie tried to hide it.

"I'm not exactly worried," Jessie said. "I'm a bit nervous, you know? I haven't seen her since

Christmas, but she's been fine on the phone and everything. It'll be easier with you here too."

It had taken Jessie a long time to understand that she wasn't the priority in her mother's life. Once she *had* really got that – her mother moving to New York without Jessie had made it pretty clear – it had taken her even longer to accept it. She thought she was pretty much there, a year later.

As she'd promised, Natalie was waiting for them at Arrivals. Jessie was quite surprised to find that she felt pleased to see her and realised that maybe she'd even missed her a little bit. She just looked so...familiar. Although she also looked thinner. And glossier.

"Wow," Emma whispered, as they approached. "She looks very 'New York'."

Jessie nodded, still staring at her mum, who was wearing loose black trousers and a (very) white shirt with flat diamante sandals and lots of silver bracelets. Her hair was lighter than it had been in England – almost blonde, in fact – and sunglasses were pushed up like a headband.

Jessie sucked her stomach in and hoped her unruly hair didn't look as ridiculous as it felt.

"Darling!" Natalie said when they finally reached her. She pulled Jessie into a hug and squeezed. "It's so good to see you."

Jessie suddenly felt a little bit tearful. To stop herself from crying she focussed on her mum's perfume. It was strange. It almost smelled like chocolate. It was kind of nice, but also a bit sickly and overwhelming.

Natalie pushed her away, still holding her with both hands on her upper arms, and smiled at Emma.

"Emma! How are you? You look lovely."

As they walked outside and Emma started telling Natalie about the flight, Jessie realised her mum hadn't told *her* that she looked lovely, just Emma. Her hair must be as bad as she feared. She pulled the bobble out and ran her hands through the tangles before putting it back in a low ponytail. She felt annoyed with herself. Why did she let her mum get to her? They hadn't even been here five minutes and she was already acting so insecure.

"Just over here for the taxis, darling," Natalie

said, gesturing across the road to a row of yellow cabs with a queue of tourists lined up on the pavement alongside them.

"Yellow cabs!" Emma said, grabbing Jessie's arm and Jessie grinned. New York. She really was in New York.

"Yes!" Natalie said as they crossed. "I was going to order a car service, but I thought you'd prefer the more authentic version. Since it's your first time here."

Natalie chattered while they waited for a taxi. About how much Jessie was going to love the apartment. About how she couldn't wait to show them New York. About how much fun they were going to have, the three of them.

But Jessie felt restless. She wanted to get to Manhattan. She'd tried to see the skyline from the plane but she'd been on the wrong side. She wanted to see the Empire State Building. And the Chrysler Building – the shiny one from the *Sex and the City* titles. She wanted to see Times Square and the Statue of Liberty. She didn't want to be standing in a queue. She could do that in England.

Eventually they were first in line and the three of them got in the back of a cab with a Yankee Stadium advert on the top.

"How long does it take?" Emma asked as the taxi pulled away from the kerb. Jessie had been about to ask the same thing.

"To the apartment?" Natalie asked. "About 40 minutes."

For all of those forty minutes Jessie stared out of the window while butterflies darted and swooped in her stomach and Emma, who was sitting in the middle, brought Natalie up to date on pretty much all her news and gossip from the past year. Jessie chimed in occasionally, but she mostly just focussed on the journey and the destination. She couldn't wait to get there, but she also wanted to remember this taxi ride. They passed apartment buildings behind wire baseball cages that made her think of *Sesame Street* and rows of small white houses like Ugly Betty's. After a little while, Jessie knew she was getting closer. To Manhattan. The buildings were getting higher, the billboards were bigger and featured video rather than just posters, but most of all, she could feel it. She could feel it bubbling up inside her.

She worried that she was building it all up too much, but she somehow felt like New York was her destiny. She believed – *she knew!* – it was where she was supposed to be and she fully expected to feel it as soon as she got there. She desperately hoped she wouldn't be disappointed. They went through a toll and then a tunnel and then she glimpsed the skyline in the distance. The Chrysler Building and the Empire State. Jessie pressed her face against the taxi window. New York. Where she was spending the summer. And where anything could happen. Anything at all.

Chapter Two

Finn was showered, dressed and ready to go when he remembered he hadn't called Scott.

He scrolled through his cell phone and called him with one hand while running the other hand through his hair. He winced at his reflection. Too much gel, but he didn't have time to do anything about it.

Scott answered with his usual, "Yeah?"

"I forgot to tell you. I won't be able to meet you before. I've got to go up to my gran's. She's having this thing."

"Jesus. Your grandmother and her things," Scott said. "But I'll probably be going straight there as well. I'll be stuck at work for the next hour at least.

The sprinklers went off and I need to wait for the guy to come and pump the place out. Jacob should be back in an hour, but I can't leave until he gets here and you know what he's like."

"I thought you were picking Sam up at the airport," Finn asked. Holding the phone between his chin and his shoulder, he wet his hands, ran them through his hair again.

"Yeah, I'm not going to get there. I've texted her, but I guess her cell's still off from the flight. She'll get it when she switches it back on."

"Right," Finn said, frowning.

"So I'll see you there later then," Scott said.

"Yeah. OK, right. Yeah," Finn said. He stuck his cell phone back in his trouser pocket then vigorously rubbed his hair with a hand towel before smoothing it back down again. Not great, but definitely better.

He grabbed his wallet and the bunch of peonies he picked up at Fairway and slammed the door behind him.

Finn had had his arm up for so long he was starting to lose feeling in his fingers. Why had he left it so late anyway? He knew what his gran was like about punctuality. She hated it when he was late and he was going to be really late if he didn't get a cab like – he checked his watch – ten minutes ago. She was going to have his balls. It was bad enough when he was late just for her, but she'd invited a friend around tonight. A Columbia professor she knew from her Amateur Dramatics club. Not one Finn was likely to have any dealings with when he got to college, but Gran had suggested he might be able to give Finn some insight into the 'Columbia experience' and what would be expected of him. Finn wasn't even slightly interested, but he knew better than to say no to his grandmother, particularly where Columbia was concerned.

Finally he saw a cab pulling up further down the block. He walked quickly towards it, trying not to break into an embarrassing jog. As he approached, the doors opened and the driver got out, followed by a glamorous woman and two cute girls who started looking around in wonder as soon as their feet hit the sidewalk.

As the driver opened the trunk and started hauling

cases out, Finn caught his eye and he nodded to confirm that, yes, he was open for another fare. Finn dodged behind the woman and almost threw himself into the cab. Sinking back against the seat, he sighed with relief. He would still be late, but at least he was on his way.

"Where to?" the cab driver asked as he got back in behind the wheel.

"80th and Lexington. Thanks."

The cab pulled out into the heavy Broadway traffic and Finn's cell phone buzzed in his pocket. It was a message from Scott.

"Alarm again. Electrical fault. Will prob b here late."

Finn put his cell back in his pocket. It wasn't like Scott to miss a gig, but if he was stuck at work, what could he do? Although Finn couldn't quite believe Scott was just going to leave Sam at the airport. Yeah, she could just get a cab, but she was expecting her boyfriend to meet her and he just wasn't going to show?

Frowning, Finn ran his hands through his hair and then shook his head briskly. He checked his watch.

"Hey? Excuse me?" He leaned forward and tapped on the scratched Perspex partition. "Could you take me to the airport instead? JFK."

When Finn had been younger, he'd fantasised about car chases, but whenever he got a New York cab, he wondered what he'd been thinking. This driver was even worst than most. Yes, he was making good time, Finn thought, as he was thrown from one side of the back seat to the other, but at what cost?

When they screeched up outside the airport, Finn felt like he'd been on the world's longest rollercoaster. His ears were ringing and he could no longer feel his thighs. He paid the driver and stepped out onto the pavement, his legs buckling briefly like he was drunk.

Dodging the tourists gathered outside the electric doors who were blinking with confusion at the rush of activity on the airport forecourt, he staggered into the building and checked the boards to find out where Sam was coming in. Sam. His grandmother was furious with him – he'd phoned her from the cab, squeezing in the call while they waited in line at the tollbooth – and all because he was picking up his best friend's girlfriend at the airport. His grandmother didn't understand. Finn wasn't entirely sure he did either.

Crossing the concourse to Arrivals, he told himself that it would have been fine if Scott had managed to speak to Sam. Finn just hated the thought that she wouldn't get the message and would be standing there alone, wondering why Scott hadn't turned up. He saw her face in his mind, full bottom lip quivering, tears balanced on the long black lashes of her beautiful blue eyes. He mentally rolled his eyes at himself. He was totally losing it.

He reached Arrivals and looked around, no sign of her. What if she'd got the message after all and grabbed a cab? How long should he wait?

"Has LA come through yet?" he asked the middle-aged woman standing next to him.

She shook her head. "No, it was delayed, apparently."

Finn stared at the double doors. Sam was somewhere on the other side. Maybe expecting Scott – her boyfriend – to be waiting, excited to see her. Or maybe she'd got the message and she was feeling disappointed, but already planning to get a cab. What she *wouldn't* be expecting was Finn. What was he thinking?! Would it be really obvious how he felt about her? At least he'd thought to leave the flowers in the cab, but do friends – just friends – turn up unannounced and unexpected to collect friends' girlfriends from the airport? Damn. He should just go. He turned and took a couple of steps.

"I think this is the LA flight now," the woman called after him.

He stopped and turned back. Waiting there for Sam could be humiliating, but Sam seeing him running away? That would be much worse.

"Thanks." He smiled at the woman and resumed staring at the door.

People piled through. Different colours, shapes, sizes. Their faces either burst into spontaneous smiles at the sight of their loved ones waiting for them or stayed in a sort of neutral sort of 'it's OK, I knew no one was collecting me' expression. And then he saw Sam and he felt like his heart was smashing against his ribs. God, she looked so completely beautiful. She was just in jeans, a plain white T-shirt, long black cardigan and no make-up, but she was still the most gorgeous girl to have come through those doors. And she was looking around. She'd stopped and was stretching up on tiptoe, obviously looking for Scott.

Finn's mouth felt dry. He licked his lips and cleared his throat, before calling, "Sam! Samantha!"

He took a few steps forward and she turned towards the sound of her name. She saw Finn and grinned. When she smiled at him like that Finn could convince himself she might have feelings for him too. He never really believed – outside his dreams and fantasises, at least – that she could possibly feel the same way about him as he did about her, but when she smiled like that, he could imagine maybe she saw him as more than just Scott's best friend.

"Hey!" she grinned and hugged him.

"Hey yourself," he said, smiling and in no way smelling her hair. He could feel her breasts pressing against his chest and he thought his knees might buckle again. That cab ride had been murder on his muscle strength.

"What are you doing here?" Sam asked, stepping back and grinning at him.

"Did you get Scott's message?"

Her eyes widened. "No! I forgot to switch my cell back on. Is he OK?"

"Yeah, yeah, he's fine. He just had to stay at work. Sprinkler emergency. Or the alarm. Or both. So—"

"So he asked you to come and get me?" Sam said, smiling. "He's such a sweetheart. And so are you. Thank you so much for coming out all this way!"

"No," Finn said. "It wasn't a problem. I couldn't leave you here on your own, could I?"

As they crossed the concourse to the exit, Sam linked her arm with Finn's and he got that feeling he always got when Sam touched him. In the base of his stomach. It was a combination of excitement at her proximity and guilt at the knowledge that he was in love with his best friend's girlfriend.

Chapter Three

Jessie stopped staring up at the beautiful building in front of her long enough to notice the boy who got into their cab. She only got a quick glimpse of him as he flung himself in the back – he must have been in a hurry – but he was definitely cute. And holding a bunch of flowers too. Maybe Emma was right about the hotness of New York boys.

"So this is home!" Natalie said, pointing up at the building.

Jessie and Emma looked up again. It really was an amazing building – covered in carvings and with tiny iron railings at each window plus a kind of turret at the corner that ran all the way down the building.

"It's fabulous," Emma said.

Jessie looked around. Apart from her mum's building, it didn't look like the most glamorous area – they were on a really busy street for one thing. And everything was just so different from home: the yellow traffic lights suspended over the street, blue post boxes, dozens of yellow taxis speeding by.

"Shall we go in?" Natalie said.

Jessie and Emma followed her through the canopied entrance and into the lobby with its black and white tiled floor and gleaming chandeliers. A man in a blue uniform pressed the lift button for them and helped them with their suitcases.

Once they were in the lift, Jessie said, "This place is amazing."

"It's lovely, isn't it," Natalie agreed. "I was so lucky to find it."

Jessie looked at her mum. It was so strange to think of her having this whole life that Jessie really knew very little about. When her mum had learned her play was going to be produced on Broadway she'd decided fairly quickly that she wanted to move there. By then, Jessie's parents had split up and

Jessie and Natalie were living in a nice – although nowhere near as nice as this – apartment in Manchester. Jessie had known her mum hadn't been entirely happy. But then Natalie told Jessie about her play transferring to Broadway and her plan to move to New York and asked her what she thought.

Jessie hadn't known what to think. She'd always been obsessed with New York. For years, it had been her dream to go there, but she'd just settled into a new school. She'd just started seeing Taylor and, at the time, thought he was the most wonderful boy she'd ever known. And she couldn't help but notice that, "Would you want to come with me?" was one of the last things her mum had said. It seemed she'd only asked her out of politeness, that she didn't really want her daughter along for the ride. So Jessie had said no. Although that didn't stop Jessie feeling shocked when her mum had actually gone. Without her.

The three of them got out of the lift, dragging their suitcases, and Natalie led them along the corridor to her apartment. Inside, it was just as gorgeous as the outside of the building had promised. They walked through a circular dining room with a small kitchen off it and into what Natalie – in a perfect French accent – called the 'pièce de resistance'. Jessie rolled her eyes, but she had to admit that her mum was right – the room was beautiful. Almost completely round, it had wood floor, a fireplace, and three huge windows – one with French doors opening onto one of the iron balconies Jessie had seen from outside.

"It's a Juliet balcony," her mum said, opening the window. "You can't go out onto it, it's just to stop you falling out of the window. There's one in your room too."

She showed them through to their room, which was a long oblong shape with two Queen-sized beds and a big window at the end. It was painted all white with wood floor and another fireplace.

"What do you think?" Natalie asked.

On the dresser between the beds was a pile of magazines – Jessie could see *People* on the top – and a huge bunch of flowers, along with a basket of American chocolate, including her favourite, Reese's Peanut Butter Cups.

"It's really great," Jessie said.

"Good." Natalie put one hand on her daughter's shoulder and gave it a squeeze. "I'll let the two of you get settled in. I'm just next door if you need me."

Emma went straight to the bathroom, but Jessie headed for the window. Opening it, she leaned out to look at the view. It overlooked the street the cab had dropped them on and a tiny park lined with trees. Jessie thought the street was probably Broadway (she'd have to ask Natalie to make sure) . Everything felt different from Manchester. The air felt different. The light looked different. She felt her eyes fill with tears. New York.

Chapter Four

Finn bought himself and Sam a coffee and they grabbed a cab back to the city.

While Sam texted Scott to tell him she'd arrived, Finn tried to think of something to talk to her about. He could ask her about her trip, obviously, but after that he was struggling. The thought of sitting in silence for the 40-minute journey was horrifying though, so he'd have to think of something.

He'd known practically everything about Samantha before he'd even met her in real life. He knew she was 5'5" tall. He knew she was a size 10, 'but curvy', Scott had said. "Like someone from *Mad Men* or something." He knew she had a step-brother named Ricky who suffered from cystic fibrosis and he knew she had an aunt living on City Island. He knew her favourite subject was English and that she wanted to work with animals. He knew she loved the singer Jason Mraz and secretly fancied Zac Efron. He knew she was allergic to dairy and addicted to sushi. He even knew – and he really wished he didn't – when her period was. He knew all this because Scott had not stopped talking about Samantha since the day he'd met her.

"So how was LA?" Finn asked, once Sam had put her cell phone back in her bag.

Sam smiled. "It was great. It's so nice to spend time with my dad with no pressure, you know?"

Finn laughed. "Not really, no."

"Oh. Is yours giving you a hard time?"

"No. It's not that so much. He doesn't really say anything, he just has all these expectations, you know? My grandmother was the same with him and he's just passing it on. But I get pressure from her too, so..." Finn shrugged.

"What about your mom?"

"She's much more easy going, yeah. Yours?"

"She's OK. She's a bit of a control freak, but she wants me to do something I'm happy with. It took her a long time to find the thing she wanted to do, so she's OK with me trying different things."

"What does she do?"

"Interior designer. What does your mom do?"

"She's a journalist: a theatre critic mainly. I think she's a frustrated playwright."

Sam laughed. "They say that about critics, don't they?"

The cab swung wildly around a bend and Finn slid sideways and up against Sam.

"Oh God! Sorry!" He dragged himself back across the seat.

She giggled. "That's OK. These cabs are lethal."

Silence. Finn stared out of the window.

"Those cages always make me think of *Sesame Street*," he said, pointing.

"Yeah?" Sam said. "I never really liked that show. I was scared of puppets and stuff when I was a kid."

"Really? God, I loved *Sesame Street*. My mom says that for a couple of years I actually thought I was Super Grover. She had to make me a cape."

Sam smiled. "Which one's Super Grover?"

"Grover? The blue one, you know?"

"I thought that was the Cookie Monster."

"Yeah, he's blue, but, no, Grover is like the skinny one... It doesn't matter."

Finn wanted to bang his head against the cab window. *I actually thought I was Super Grover?!* What was he thinking?!

"Are you going to this gig with Scott tonight?" Sam asked.

"Yeah. If he gets off work."

"I said I'd go too, but I'm too exhausted. I've been up for... What time is it now?"

Finn checked his watch. "Nine."

Sam's eyes widened. "Wow, really? Um...I can't work it out, but it's a long time. I'm beat."

Finn just nodded.

"That job's turning into a bit of a nightmare for Scott. He's having to do a lot more hours than he signed up for."

"It's just that the sprinkler went off, I think," Finn said. "I don't think he would've offered to stay if Jacob'd been around."

"Yeah, but he covers for people a lot. And he's doing all this overtime, you know."

"Right."

Finn didn't understand why Scott was working so much. The deli was just supposed to be a stop-gap, part time job, so why was Scott letting it get so out of hand? Unless. Finn glanced over at Sam. She was biting her thumbnail. He'd noticed her doing that before. Only her thumbnail, though: the rest of her nails weren't bitten.

Finn frowned. Scott had screwed around on girlfriends in the past, Finn knew, but he didn't think he'd do that to Sam. Scott was mad about Sam, wasn't he? Yeah, he'd let her down tonight, but Finn had thought that was a one-off, not that he was cheating on her or losing interest.

What if he was? What if Scott broke up with her? Would Finn be able to ask her out? No. She'd still be off-limits, surely. You don't date your best friend's ex, do you?

"Are you OK?" Sam asked.

Finn flinched, afraid for a second he'd been muttering out loud. "Yeah, no, I'm fine. Sorry. Miles away."

***

As the cab pulled up outside Sam's apartment building near Washington Square, Finn saw Scott standing underneath the awning. He moved forward to open the cab door and then frowned when he saw Finn sat alongside Sam. "Hey, man."

"Hey," Finn said. He felt sick. He shouldn't have gone to the airport. It was weird. Scott would know he liked Sam. It was obvious. Sam probably knew too. Oh God.

"Do you want to come in?" Sam asked Finn, once she'd finished kissing her boyfriend.

Finn glanced at Scott, who was looking at him funny, although he didn't seem to be annoyed. He did, however, seem to be trying to convey that he hadn't seen Sam for ten days and so Finn would not be welcome.

"No," Finn said, leaning out of the cab's door. "Thanks, but I'll let you two catch up."

Scott and Sam both grinned at him and he smiled back, weakly. Scott slammed the door and the cab pulled away from the kerb.

Chapter Five

"Can you believe we're waking up in New York?" Jessie said, lying on her back and staring up at the bright, white ceiling.

A "mumphurgh" sound emerged from under the duvet on Emma's bed.

"Emma!" Jessie said. "We're in NEW YORK, baby! Wake up!"

Emma pushed the duvet off her face and frowned across at her friend. "I feel like I've only just fallen asleep."

"Pfft," Jessie said, grinning at her friend's creased face and bed head. "You've been snoring for hours."

"We were *talking* for hours," Emma said, rolling

onto her stomach and pushing herself up on her elbows. "What time did we go to sleep? Two?"

"I don't know," Jessie said. "It's eight now though, so get up."

"Eight?! What time's that at home?"

"Who cares? We're here now!"

"Wake me at 11," Emma mumbled, turning her back on Jessie and pulling the duvet over her head.

"No!" Jessie said. She sat up and swung her legs out of bed. "New York! We have to go and explore!"

"You go and explore. Come back and tell me all about it. Take pictures."

"I'm going for a shower," Jessie said. "You'd better be up when I get back."

Jessie opened the bedroom door, peered out and then padded through to the lounge and diner, but there was no sign of Natalie.

"Mum?" Jessie said.

No reply.

Maybe she'd gone out. Or maybe she was still in bed, it *was* pretty early after all. Jessie knocked on her mum's bedroom door and then, when there was no response, pushed it open. Empty. And the king-sized bed was already made.

Jessie realised her mum hadn't shown her the next room – she knew immediately what it would be: her office. Jessie knocked twice, but hearing nothing, pushed the door open, saying "Mum?" as she opened it.

She heard a little tut of impatience before she was fully in the room, but then her mum recovered herself enough to say, "Just bear with me a sec, I'm just in the middle..."

She briefly swung round in her chair and smiled that distracted smile Jessie knew so well, before turning back to the computer.

Jessie stood and waited for her mum, much like she'd been doing for as long as she could remember. When she was younger, when her parents were still together, there were so many times Jessie had gone into her mum's office – which, at that time, had been a glorified cupboard under the stairs, lit with fairy lights and with an ancient computer balanced on an Ikea stool – and Natalie wouldn't even notice she was there. Jessie would often stand there saying, "Mum. Mum. Mum. Mum," over and over until

Natalie finally realised and, more often than not, snapped "What, Jess?!" without taking her eyes off the computer screen. Her mum and dad used to argue about it, but in reality her dad wasn't much better. He was building up his architecture practice and hardly ever around.

Eventually, in her early teens, Jessie learned to use it to her advantage. Just one "Mum?" followed by a request and it was always granted. Natalie never listened, she just agreed to whatever it was in order to get Jessie to go away. That's how Jessie and Emma ended up getting the bus to the Trafford Centre when they were eleven. How they got bought tickets to see My Chemical Romance when they were 12. How Jessie got her ears pierced. Eventually Jessie realised that she didn't even need to ask her mum, she could just tell her that she had. It was all the same.

After a couple of minutes, Jessie's mum swung round again and said, "Sorry about that. And good morning! Did you sleep well?"

Jessie nodded. Her mum didn't look nearly as groomed and glossy as she had the previous day,

Jessie noticed. Her hair was tied up in a messy bun and she was wearing her glasses, a shabby-looking pink T-shirt and what looked like tracksuit bottoms.

"So this is my office," she said. "I didn't show you yesterday, did I?"

The office was small but bright, with another large window, wood floor and a fireplace. The walls were white apart from one alcove that was covered in red and white striped wallpaper and framed reviews.

Natalie pointed at a framed copy of Playbill featuring her show, *Small Change*.

"I sent you a Playbill, didn't I?" she asked.

Jessie nodded. The small programme for the play had lived on her bedside table for a while, but now it was in a drawer.

Next to the window Jessie noticed a tiny shelf with a couple of framed photographs. She squinted. The photos were of her. There was one of her and her mum, taken when Jessie was about six. She and Natalie had their arms around each other and their hair was messy as if it had been windy. Natalie looked beautiful and was smiling straight into the camera. Jessie was looking off to the side.

"Where was that taken?" Jessie asked her mum.

"That one?" Natalie asked, pointing at the other photo, which was Jessie on her own, standing in their old hallway and cuddling their old cat, Mufti, who'd been run over just before they'd moved to Manchester.

"No." Jessie pointed. "That one."

"Oh! That was taken on the beach at Caernarfon. Do you remember that holiday?"

"Not much, no," Jessie said.

All she remembered about that holiday was walking on the beach with her dad. In fact, whenever she'd thought about the holiday she hadn't been entirely sure her mum had even been there.

"That's where I first started writing *Small Change*," Natalie said and Jessie almost laughed. She'd been touched when she saw the photos of herself on the shelf, she should have known at least one of them was more to remind Natalie of her dreams coming true than of the daughter she left behind.

"I'm going for a shower," Jessie said.

Natalie had already turned back to the computer,

her fingers hovering over the keyboard. "OK," she said.

Jessie dropped her pyjamas on the floor of the green-tiled bathroom, turned on the taps – which, brilliantly, had a temperature setting (so much more sensible than the little bit of hot, little bit of cold method she had to employ when showering at home) – and climbed under the gushing water.

She hadn't realised her mum had started writing her play so long ago. She hadn't finished it until probably around the time of the other photograph, maybe a bit earlier, when Jessie was about 12 or 13. Her mum had been doing a screenwriting course in the evenings and the tutor, Jack, thought her play was brilliant.

He'd helped her mum produce *Small Change* at a small local theatre. She was always going out for dinner with him and she spoke to him on the phone at least twice a day, often more. Jessie was forever walking into rooms to find her mum whispering and giggling on the phone. She wanted to warn her dad – it made her laugh to think of it now – she wanted to warn him about Jack, that her mum was spending so much time with him while John was at work. That she'd lost weight and had started dressing differently and spending more time on her hair and make-up.

But it had been her dad who'd broken up the family. He was the one who'd fallen in love with someone else. He was the one who ended the marriage. But he hadn't moved to the other side of the world, had he? No, unlike Natalie, he'd managed to completely change his life without leaving Jessie behind.

Chapter Six

Finn braved the subway and met Scott and Sam at their favourite café on LaGuardia Place. They were sitting outside in the sun and Sam was wearing a mini skirt and flip-flops with a tight tee. Finn tried not to look at her legs and sat down opposite her.

"You didn't go last night then?" Scott asked him.

Finn shook his head. "Nah, man. I just went home."

After dropping Sam off with Scott, he hadn't been able to face going back downtown for the gig. It wasn't a band he was really into anyway; they were more Scott's thing. His mom and dad had been out seeing a play, so he'd watched *Independence Day* on cable, and felt sorry for himself.

"You'll never believe what I'm going to be doing this summer," Sam said. "The letter was waiting for me when I got home."

"What?" Finn asked.

"Central Park Zoo! They're running a work-study programme. I've always wanted to work at the zoo."

"You're kidding?!" Finn said and then laughed. "You might get to work with Alex the Lion."

"Who's Alex the Lion?" Sam asked.

"You don't know Alex the Lion?" Finn asked. "He's in *Madagascar.*"

"The country?"

"No. The movie. You know?"

"Oh! I haven't seen it." Sam said. "Aren't you a bit old for cartoons?"

"Nope. Never too old for cartoons. You like *The Simpsons*, don't you?"

Sam wrinkled her nose.

"You don't like *The Simpsons*?"

"It's a cartoon!" Sam said.

"Right," Finn said. "So. If you're not going to be

working with Alex the Lion – you know, cos he's animated and everything – what are you going to be doing?"

"Oh, a lot of it will be cleaning and admin and that kind of thing, but I should get to work with the animals a little too."

"I just hope it's less of a pain in the ass than my job right now," Scott said.

"Oh my God!" Sam said, her face lighting up. "You should sign up too!"

"The zoo?" Scott pulled a horrified face. "I can't stand the zoo."

"Scott's scared of penguins," Finn said.

"I'm not *scared* of them," Scott said. "They just creep me out. They don't blink."

"Yeah," Finn said, "And the ones in *Madagascar* built a plane. Who knows what they're capable of?"

Sam laughed. "What about you?" she asked Finn. "Why don't you do it? It'll be fun!"

"Nah, I've got to go work for my dad," Finn said, although the thought of spending the summer with Sam made his stomach clench. "It's possible that I will actually die of boredom."

"So why are you doing it?" Scott asked, fiddling with his Blackberry.

Finn shrugged. "I promised my dad."

"He'd understand."

"If I went to work at the zoo? I don't think so."

"It doesn't have to be the zoo. I could get you a job with me," Scott said. "God knows we need the help. Or you could find something you're actually, you know, *interested* in."

"Yeah," Finn said. "I dunno. I'm gonna see how it goes."

"What does your dad do?" Sam asked.

"Insurance."

"But you're not interested in insurance, are you?"

Finn shook his head. "Not really. But it's not meant to be about that. It's about showing me a 9–5, work ethics, business practices and all that."

"So you do want to go into business?" Sam asked. "Doing what?"

"I don't know," Finn said. "That's pretty much the problem."

"What are you majoring in?"

Scott snorted and Finn said, "Business."

Even Sam pulled a face. "Why? If that's not what you want to do?"

"Because it's a good foundation for whatever I do decide I want to do."

"I don't know." Sam shook her head. "I just can't see you being one of those Wall Street guys, with the suit and the frown..." She reached out and touched Finn's forehead just above the bridge of his nose.

"I can't either, man," Scott said as Finn tried to catch his breath and, at the same time, capture the feeling of Sam touching his face so he could remember it later. At home. Alone.

Finn asked, "What *do* you see me doing?"

"Something more creative," Sam said.

"Something more relaxed," Scott said.

"Relaxed and creative?" Finn asked, grinning. "That's the best you've got?"

"What did you want to be when you were a child?" Sam asked.

"A Power Ranger," Finn and Scott both said at the same time.

Sam rolled her eyes. "You know? Race car driver? Firefighter?"

"Ballerina?" Scott added.

Finn looked at his friends and said, "Architect." He pushed his metal chair back and stood up. "I'm gonna get a coffee. You want anything?"

"Could I get another of these?" Sam asked, gesturing at her glass. "Mango iced tea?"

Finn nodded.

"Yeah, same again," Scott said, pointing at his espresso cup.

"Right," Finn said. He pushed open the door and stepped into the tiny café. It was so tiny that he was at the counter with two steps.

The owner, Anne-Marie, grinned at him, as she arranged muffins on a cake stand. "Back again?"

Finn smiled. "Yep. Can't keep us away."

"Do you live round here too?"

"No. I live uptown. Sam lives just round the corner." He gestured through the window and glanced out to see Sam and Scott were kissing.

"So they make you come all the way down here?" Anne-Marie asked. She put a dome over the top of the cakes and then added, "You're a good friend."

Finn laughed. "No, I come here for the best coffee."

"And for that, you can have a muffin on the house!" She took a muffin out and put it on a plate with a knife and a paper napkin. "What can I get you?"

When he got back outside, Sam was gone.

"Vintage store," Scott said, pointing across the road.

Finn put the drinks down on the table and sat down. Closing his eyes, he tipped his head back and felt the sun on his face.

"Hey," Scott said. "Thanks for picking Sam up from the airport."

Finn snapped his head back down and opened his eyes. Scott was looking at him, a slight frown on his face.

"Yeah," Finn said. He rubbed the back of his neck. "It was weird, wasn't it? I know. I just... I got in the cab to go to my gran's and, I dunno, I just couldn't face it. And then I remembered Sam was at the airport and it just seemed like...it seemed like the right thing to do, you know?"

"Right. Well, thanks, man. I appreciate it. So does Sam."

Finn took a gulp of his coffee, which was much too hot.

"Did you get things sorted?" he asked Scott. "At work?"

"Oh yeah. It was a mess. You know, everything got soaked, we had to throw a load of stuff out, but it should be OK."

"So it's going well, yeah?" Finn said. "You and Sam?"

"It's great," Scott said. "You like her, right?"

Finn glanced at his friend to make sure he knew exactly what he was asking and then he said, "Yeah. She's cool."

Chapter Seven

Jessie had showered and then finally convinced Emma to get out of bed and into the bathroom to shower. Then the two of them had coaxed Natalie out of her office and *she'd* showered.

"If it takes us this long to get ready every day we're not going to see much of New York," Jessie said, sitting at the dining table and flicking through a copy of *New York* magazine.

"Where do you want to go?" Natalie asked. She was standing in front of the mirror putting on mascara and holding her mouth in a really weird way.

"Where do you suggest?" Emma said. "Take us to your favourite place!"

"NOT the theatre!" Jessie said, without looking up from the magazine.

Her mum laughed. "No, not today, darling."

She did the other eye and then said, "I know exactly where we should go!"

Before she could elaborate she disappeared into her bedroom and Emma said to Jessie, "You seem to be getting on OK."

"Yeah. I promised Dad I'd try not to be, you know, a complete bitch."

Jessie and Emma grinned at each other.

"She's obviously trying though," Emma said. "Don't you think?"

"Yeah, I suppose. I don't know. It seems really weird. I've got used to it just being me and dad, you know? It seems mad to suddenly have a mum again."

"You've always had a mum," Emma said.

"Yeah, on the end of the phone once a week. Or in an occasional email—"

"She sent you that Cover Girl stuff," Emma interrupted.

"Yeah," Jessie said. "Most of which you pinched.

I know she's my mum. It's just going to take a bit of time to get used to her again, I think."

Natalie came back in, smiling smugly.

"Where are we going?" Emma asked.

"You'll see..."

The heat hit them as soon as they pushed open the main doors and stepped out on to the street. It was like opening an oven door.

"Woah!" Jessie said.

"Yeah," Natalie said, smiling. "This is why New York empties in the summer."

They turned right and headed down the main street.

"So this is Broadway," Natalie said, as they walked.

"I thought it was!" Jessie said. "When I looked out the window."

"So your play's on Broadway and you live on Broadway?" Emma said. "That's pretty cool!"

"It is," Natalie agreed, smiling. "It's pretty cool."

Emma nudged Jessie and pointed to a branch of Abercrombie & Fitch right there, on the same block as Natalie's building. On the opposite site of the road was the park Jessie had seen out of the window.

"What's that?" she asked.

"Verdi Square. The 72nd Street subway is there – I'll show you when we cross. It'll take you to Times Square, Wall Street, the Village, right down to the ferry. I do yoga down there." She pointed down a side street and then led Jessie and Emma across to the subway at the other end of the park.

"Is the subway safe?" Emma asked.

"Yes. It can be a bit grotty – I wouldn't use it late at night – but it's fine during the day...although in this heat it's very sweaty."

"I'll show you how to find your way around. Manhattan is mostly a grid. The avenues run top to bottom and so does Broadway. Then the streets run across. So that's 72nd, which means that way – north..." she pointed, "...will be 73rd and that way – south – is 71st. So if you get lost and don't know which way you're going, you only need to walk one block to work it out."

Jessie and Emma looked at her blankly and she laughed. "You'll get used to it really quickly, I promise."

They crossed another main road – Jessie and Emma gawping at a glinting glass cube of a building on the corner – and then walked down 72nd street.

"So now we're heading west," Natalie said. "If you think of the park in the middle, the streets to the right of the park are east and to the left are west. The park is north and the tip – the ferry and the Statue of Liberty – are south."

"We'll get used to it," Jessie said to Emma and they both grinned.

As they walked, Natalie told them about moving to New York. How Jack had helped her find her apartment because he'd lived there a few years earlier and knew his way around. He'd shown her the Upper West Side first because it was his favourite area and she'd loved it straight away.

"Where does Jack live?" Jessie asked, nudging Emma as they passed a fabulous looking vintage shop.

"Not far from me," Natalie said and Jessie raised her eyebrows at Emma. "But up towards Riverside Drive."

Natalie told Emma – Jessie already knew – how

she'd moved into a smaller place in the same building when she'd first come to New York. "But then mine became available. I just went to look out of nosiness really, but I fell in love with it," Natalie said. "I knew I had to have it and then I sold the film rights, so..."

"You sold the film rights?" Emma said.

Natalie nodded. "Yes. I doubt anything will come of it. People buy the rights all the time, but not many movies actually get made."

"But you get to keep the money?" Jessie asked.

"Yep."

"Cool."

They crossed another main road – Columbus Avenue, Natalie told them – and then crossed the side street too and carried on walking down 72nd Street, looking up at the buildings and getting excited about apartment buildings with doormen and canopies.

"I looked at an apartment in here," Natalie said, pointing up at a brown brick building. "It was a bit dingy. And expensive."

"How much do they cost?" Emma asked.

"Well the one I looked at in there was $6000, but it was a one-bedroom."

"Six thousand dollars?" Emma said. "For how long?"

"A month," Natalie said and Emma and Jessie stared at each other, wide-eyed.

"We should have a talk about pocket money," Jessie said, smiling.

Her mum laughed. "Yeah. Maybe we should."

As they approached the end of the road, Jessie said, "Is that Central Park?" There was another main road, but on the other side of it, all they could see was trees.

"Yes," Natalie said, "But I wanted to show you this building first." She pointed at the building opposite. It looked a bit like a fairytale castle with its turrets and round bay windows.

"That's the Dakota," Natalie said. "It's one of the most famous buildings in New York. John Lennon lived there."

"And died there, right?" Jessie said.

Her mum nodded.

"So sad," Jessie said.

"I remember when it happened," Natalie said. "Your gran really loved him – she was a big Beatles fan – and I saw it on the front page of the paper and showed her. And she burst into tears. I felt awful."

"He sang *Imagine*, yeah?" Emma said. "We sang that at the leavers' assembly at primary school."

"I remember," Natalie said. "I cried so much I thought I was going to be sick."

Jessie laughed. "Did you? I don't remember that!"

"God, it was AWFUL! I couldn't look at your dad because I knew he'd start crying too..." As she talked she led them over to cross the main road towards the park. "I got that pain in my throat – you know the one you get when you're trying not to cry?" They crossed the road. "I knew I was going to let out a massive sob and so I went and hid in the loos."

They stopped in front of an ice-cream stall and Natalie said, "Ice cream?"

The girls nodded and Natalie went to buy ice cream for the three of them.

"I didn't know she went to the loos to cry," Jessie said to Emma. "I remember seeing her leaving and I thought she'd just got bored or something."

"Really?" Emma said.

"Yeah. I didn't speak to her for the rest of the day."

"Wow."

"I know."

Jessie looked at her mum, buying the ice creams and flirting with the vendor. Funny, she'd held that against her for years. And now she had to let it go.

They walked through the park eating their ice creams and – Jessie and Emma, at least – exclaiming at everything. It was so strange to find such a beautiful park in the middle of such a crazy-busy city. Although the park wasn't exactly quiet. People were running, roller-skating, even horse-riding. And people in rickshaws being pulled by cyclists passed them more than once.

"We have got to have a go in one of them!" Jessie said.

"No way," her mum said. "Much too dangerous."

They approached a terrace and Jessie suddenly squealed. "Look! It's the place from *One Fine Day*!"

"Is it?" Emma said.

"Yes!" Jessie headed down the steps with Emma

and Natalie behind her. "You remember? The kids run into the puddle and then George Clooney picks her up and splashes around."

"Oh yeah!" Emma grinned. "Shame there's no puddle."

"Shame there's no George Clooney," Natalie said.

At the bottom of the steps, they crossed the terrace towards the lake.

"That's where we're going," Natalie said, pointing across the water at the Boathouse Café.

"Oh my God!" Jessie yelled.

"Good choice?" Natalie asked, laughing.

"Great choice." Jessie grinned at her mum, who smiled right back.

They sat on the terrace. Closing her eyes, Jessie tipped her head back and felt the sun on her face. She was in New York. And not just New York, but Central Park. And not just Central Park, but the Boathouse Café, setting of one of the scenes from her favourite film of all time: *When Harry Met Sally*.

She had an urge to send Taylor a text – something

to let him know she was fine without him, wasn't even thinking about him, but she knew that if she did that, he'd know it wasn't true. She sat on her hands and waited for the feeling to pass.

"So this is the scene when...?" she heard her mum ask and she opened her eyes to answer.

"When Sally tells her friends that she's split up with Joe and Marie looks through that address thing?"

"Rolodex," her mum said.

"Ooh!" Emma said, "It was in *27 Dresses* too."

"I haven't seen that," Natalie said. "Is it good?"

While Emma told Jessie's mum about the film – Jessie hadn't seen it either – Jessie thought about how she and her mum had used to watch rom-coms together on a Sunday afternoon. Some weeks it was the only time they spent together.

Emma and Natalie were interrupted in their mutual admiration of James Marsden by the waiter asking for their order. They had a quick look at the menu and ordered French toast, bacon, tea and orange juice and then carried on talking about their favourite films set in New York.

"You've seen *Manhattan*, right? With Woody Allen?" Natalie asked them.

"I've seen it," Jessie said. "But not with Woody Allen. Dad doesn't let me hang out with him anymore."

"Ha ha," Natalie said, grinning. "And *Annie Hall*, of course. In fact you two should do one of the movie tours. You know? They take you to the locations of lots of films and TV shows."

"There's a tour just on *Sex and the City*, isn't there?" Emma asked.

"There are lots of different ones, I think," Natalie said. "Have you thought about what else you'd like to do?"

"*All* the tourist stuff," Jessie said.

"And shopping," Emma added.

"And the museums?" Natalie suggested.

"Oh yeah, obviously," Jessie said, smiling. "We wouldn't miss the museums."

Her eyes crinkling against the sun, Jessie's mum smiled at them both. "We're going to have such a good time."

Chapter Eight

Finn had grown up on the Upper East Side. Not with an obviously affluent address. Not with an address that would immediately mark him out as New York Royalty or anything. But still, the Upper East Side was the Upper East Side. But then, Finn had got into the school he and his parents had loved and the school was on the opposite side of the park. At the same time, by coincidence or, as his mom preferred to think of it, providence, an apartment had become available in a classic building, a building his parents had admired for years and which was in walking distance of his new school. So they'd moved to the Upper West Side.

They'd never regretted it – Finn's parents were totally and utterly in love with their historical and "architecturally important" Art Deco home, and Finn loved his school as much as it was possible to love somewhere it was compulsory to attend five days a week – but the main thing was, they turned out to be very much more Upper West Side people than Upper East Side people.

When Finn went back there to visit his grandmother, he couldn't quite believe they'd ever fitted in. It wasn't just the money aspect; Upper East Siders seemed to be a different breed. Rich, yes, but also privileged. Often spoiled and with a sense of entitlement...well, everyone had seen *Gossip Girl* and it wasn't far-fetched. If anything, they underplayed it. Finn had heard stuff about Upper East Side girls he'd previously gone to school with that they'd baulk at showing on HBO, never mind The CW.

The Upper West Side, in contrast, was a bit *crunchier*. A bit more eco-friendly, at least as much as you could be in a city like New York. Some of the shops were co-ops, some of the people wore hemp.

The stores sold more organic cous cous and less caviar. Finn loved it.

One of the best things about where they lived was the deli downstairs. Finn's mother barely ate anything – she wasn't anorexic or anything, she was just one of those weird people who were almost completely disinterested in food – and consequently often forgot to buy any. Finn's father usually picked stuff up on the way home from work, but he tended to stick to coffee and cigarettes in the morning, so breakfast foods were usually in short supply. Finn, when he remembered, picked up bagels or doughnuts, but he often didn't bother, preferring to have an excuse to pop downstairs to Gino's for an omelette or sausage and egg bagel.

"How you doin'?" Gino asked in a manner that always reminded Finn of Joey from *Friends*, but it wasn't meant to be a come-on. Not to him anyway.

"Good, man, thanks," Finn said.

"Usual?" Gino asked.

"Great," Finn said. The usual was a bacon and mushroom omelette and a black coffee. His mom would be horrified if she knew he was drinking black coffee, but that was the way Finn's father had always drunk it and Finn had been sneaking sips of it for as long as he could remember. The first time he'd been disgusted and had run to the bathroom to guzzle water from the faucet to get rid of the taste, but that hadn't stopped him trying it again and again. Now he almost found it pleasant. Almost, but not quite. It still reminded him faintly of the smell of melting asphalt, but it *was* the best way he'd found to wake him up for the day.

Gino put the coffee down on the table and asked, "What ya doin' today?"

"I'm starting a summer job with my dad," Finn said and grinned. "At the Empire State Building."

"Cool!" Gino said, his round face lighting up. "I love that place!"

"Me too," Finn said. "Not so sure about the job. Insurance."

Gino swore beneath his breath and then said, as he always did, "Scuse my language." He paused. "You wanna work here? I need a dishwasher..."

Finn grinned. "Thanks. I'll keep it in mind."

"Insurance not looking so bad now, eh?" Laughing,

he went back round behind the counter and Finn stared out of the window, watching New York wake up and, as so often these days, thinking about Sam.

She'd looked so beautiful last night. She always did. But the thing about Sam was that she was sweet too. She wasn't like the girls Finn had been at school with. Those girls knew they were gorgeous and looked at Finn like he should be grateful they were giving him their attention. They were so full of themselves. But Sam was enthusiastic and friendly and down-to-earth. And it's not as if Finn was bad-looking himself. He was no Jared Leto, but he was OK.

Sam and Scott had seemed so happy when Finn had dropped her off. Maybe Scott wasn't messing around after all. Maybe. Finn would be kind of surprised if he was, because Scott had had plenty of girlfriends before but he'd never known him to fall as hard as he had for Sam.

Finn had known Scott for his entire life. Or as much of it as he could remember anyway. His mother and Scott's mother were friends and so he and Scott played together as babies, went to the same preschool, elementary school, high school. In fact, they'd seen each other every day until Scott had started dating Sam.

But then the three of them had started hanging out and the more time Finn spent with Samantha, the more envious he became of Scott. But she was Scott's girlfriend. Finn knew she was out of bounds. Far out of bounds.

"How you doin'?" the guy behind the counter asked and Jessie and Emma both laughed. He didn't look like Joey Tribbiani. Maybe Joey's dad.

Natalie had stepped out of her office long enough this morning to give the girls details of the tour she'd booked (along with some cash and an emergency credit card – apparently they could use someone else's credit card here, no problems) and to suggest the girls get breakfast at the deli downstairs.

"We're really good, thank you," Emma said.

"Where you girls from?" 'Joey's dad' asked them.

"England," Jessie said. But England felt very far away.

"Ah!" he said, "You like David Beckham?"

Jessie and Emma both laughed. "Yes!"

"He's a hottie, right?"

They both laughed again.

"So what'll ya have?" Joey's dad asked.

"Oh!" Jessie stared up at the menu boards above the counter. There was too much choice. Eggs five different ways. Home fries. Omelettes. Pancakes. She wanted to try everything.

"Oh God," Jessie said. "Pancakes! Please."

"With everything?"

"Yes," Jessie said.

Emma ordered eggs and toast, while Jessie looked around for a table. A guy sitting in the window was just getting up to leave so Jessie took a step closer to make sure she got it as soon as he went. He turned and Jessie realised he was much younger than she'd thought. And really cute, with fantastic cheekbones.

"Hi," he said.

Well she was standing pretty close.

She smiled and watched him leave and only as the door closed behind him did she realise she hadn't said anything back.

"Phwoar," Emma said as they sat down.

"I know," Jessie said. "I made a tit out of myself though. Shock."

"Ah, but it's baby steps. After a break-up, it always takes a while to get back on the horse. At least you recognised a hot boy. After Taylor you said you'd never look at another boy again."

"But that was before I knew I was coming to New York."

"True. I'm thinking a hot New York boy is exactly what you need."

"Agreed," Jessie said and then smiled. "You think we'll meet one on the..." She checked the ticket. "... New York TV and Movie Tour?"

"I very much doubt it."

Jessie looked at the time on the ticket. "Mum said it's about ten minutes walk from here, so we'll need to leave by quarter past ten."

Their breakfasts arrived. Jess's was a stack of pancakes about four inches high, dusted with icing sugar, next to which was a sausage, two pieces of bacon, a pile of fried potatoes and another pile of strawberries and blueberries. The Joey's dad guy also put down a small jug. "Maple syrup," he told her and winked.

"Oh my God!" Emma said.

Jessica stared at her plate. Aside from the idea that bacon and strawberries and sausages and blueberries and fried potatoes and maple syrup didn't go together in any way, it looked like one of the most delicious breakfasts Jessie had ever seen. The pancakes weren't like the kind of pancakes she was used to having on Shrove Tuesday, these were thick and fluffy and, when she cut into them with her fork, absolutely delicious. She tried a bit with some bacon and then some sausage and then some fruit. Delicious. She poured the maple syrup over the top of everything. Emma just watched her.

"Syrup with sausage?!" Emma said eventually, screwing up her nose.

"I know. It sounds disgusting, but Americans know food," Jessie smiled. She piled a bit of everything – well, as much as she could fit – on her fork and almost moaned. It was amazing.

"Good?" Emma asked.

"Amazing," Jessie said.

Emma reached over and helped herself, before moaning along with Jess. "Bloody hell. Let's never go home."

"I've been thinking about that," Jessie said.

"What?"

"Never going home."

"What, seriously?"

"Yeah. I mean, I could go home and go to sixth form and then maybe go to university here or I could just, you know, finish school here."

"And live with your mum?"

"Well I'd have to, yeah."

"Can you do that?"

"I don't know, but I'm definitely thinking about looking into it. You know at university here you don't have to pick just one thing? You can do a lot of different subjects and then choose something to, like, specialise in later."

"Yeah, I know. But do you think you're ready for that?"

"Well, yeah," Jessie said. "It makes sense, doesn't it? I don't want to pick a degree course and then get stuck doing something I hate or I'm not good at. It's

OK for people like you who know what they want to do..."

Emma had wanted to be a teacher for as long as she could remember.

"No, you're right," Emma said. "Like a try before you buy type of thing. But I meant are you ready to live with your mum?"

"Oh right!" Jessie shook her head. "Not yet, no. I mean, I'm not sure yet. She might not even want me to, you know? But I'm thinking about it. How amazing would it be to live here?!"

Shoving more of Jess's pancake in her mouth, Emma nodded.

"It would be totally amazing," she said. "And I can do a year in America as part of my degree – maybe I could even go to the same uni as you?"

"Yes!" Jessie said, grinning. "God, that would be so good."

Emma's toast and eggs 'over easy' were completely forgotten as the two friends systematically ate their way through pretty much everything on Jessie's plate and talked about how cool it would be to share a New York apartment, if only for a year.

"We'd better go," Jessie said, noticing the time.

"Can we take this with us?" Emma joked, standing and picking up her bag, before shoving one last forkful of potatoes into her mouth.

"You like that, huh?" the guy came over to clear the table and Jessie smiled at him.

"It was delicious," Jessie said. "Thank you so much."

"Want me to put that in a box for yus?" he asked, nodding at the remaining potato, piece of bacon and pancake.

Jessie saw Emma's eyes light up, but what were they going to do? Eat it on the coach?

"No," she said. "Thank you though. We'll definitely be back."

Chapter Nine

Finn walked the two blocks across to Central Park West, wearing his iPod and dodging the business people and tourists who'd started to take over the sidewalks. It was a beautiful day – blue sky, sun shining, but not too humid. In fact, it was such a great day he was beginning to wish he'd thought to run to work and change when he got there. His dad thought he was crazy for walking instead of getting a cab or the subway, but he was in no hurry – his dad had a morning meeting so he had told Finn any time before lunch was fine.

And witnessing New York waking up was one of the very best things about living there. It wasn't exactly quiet – New York was never quiet – but there was a different atmosphere. The streets were emptier and there was an air of expectation. The pavements were wet from the street cleaners and even the drivers were more relaxed; there was much less honking and screeching of tyres.

He couldn't quite believe he was on his way to work at the Empire State Building. Finn had been eight years old when his father's company had relocated there. He'd been ridiculously excited because he didn't quite understand that, just because his dad worked there, it didn't mean he was going to spend any time there. He hadn't been more than once a year for the past ten years. When he did go, he got to skip the tourist lines and go straight to the top, but only when his dad was with him and his dad was usually too busy for that. In fact, moving to such a prestigious address had come at a time of growth for the firm and so Charles – Finn's father – was used to working 18-hour days.

Between visits to the Empire State, Finn read up about it. His teachers had teased him at school because whenever the children could choose their own project, Finn picked some aspect of the Empire State.

"There's a lot more to New York than that one building," they used to say. Or "There's a big world outside New York, you know?" but Finn wasn't interested. The Empire State Building fascinated him. He loved the story about the pole to tether zeppelins, but more than that he loved stories about the people who worked there. Before 9/11 one of his favourite stories had been about a plane crashing into the top of the building, but he didn't enjoy that one so much anymore.

Finn always thought the Empire State Building would be the perfect place for a date (not just a meeting, like in *An Affair to Remember* – one of his gran's favourite movies – or *Sleepless in Seattle*, which was one of his mom's, but a proper date), if only there was a bit more room on the viewing platform. It needed a restaurant or something so you could take full advantage of the view.

Finn's grandmother had known a man who'd worked at the Empire State Building during the war.

He'd told her stories, which she'd passed on to Finn. Stories of secretaries leaning out of the window to smoke, tipping up and being pulled back in by their ankles. It all seemed so glamorous. New York was still glamorous, of course, but it was a flashy *Gossip Girl* kind of glamour. Finn preferred the idea of old glamour. Old New York. Delmonico's and Automats.

Finn's stomach rumbled and he stopped to buy a pretzel from a cart at Columbus Circle. He felt positive. The sun was shining, he had a hot, soft, salted pretzel, and he was on his way to work in his favourite building in the world.

Jessica and Emma waited at the stop for the bus tour to arrive. They'd expected there to be a queue, but they were the only people waiting...until a couple of minutes before the coach arrived when a crowd of tourists seemed to appear out of nowhere.

The coach – with its New York Movie Tour logo painted on the side – pulled up and everyone clambered on and found their seats.

"Are you ready for this tour?" the tour guide asked and then, when she didn't get quite the response she obviously expected, she repeated, "ARE YOU READY TO HAVE FUN?!"

Jessie and Emma looked at one another and laughed. They totally were.

Three hours later, they'd seen the deli from *When Harry Met Sally*, the restaurant where Tom Hanks spit the caviar out in *Big*, the bookshop from *You've Got Mail*, Monica's restaurant from *Friends*, Grace's office from *Will & Grace*, the firehouse from *Ghostbusters*, the Cosby house and, as an added bonus, Monica Lewinsky's apartment. There'd been questions asked about each of the stops and Jessie had surprised herself by getting lots of them right. The tour guide awarded a lollipop for correct answers and, by the end of the tour, when they were dropped back uptown, Jessie had six and Emma had one (for knowing that the 'I'll have what she's having' woman in *When Harry Met Sally* was the film's director – Rob Reiner's – mother).

They'd been dropped off downtown and so decided to walk back to Natalie's building to help them get an idea of the city. They could take Broadway the entire way, which thrilled them both. Emma had been singing 'Give My Regards to Broadway' since they'd got off the bus and had started looking for somewhere to get something to eat.

"Ooh!" Jessie said, suddenly. "Let's get pretzels!"

Emma pulled a face. "I don't think I like them."

"Well you get a hotdog then and you can always try a bit of mine."

They ended up buying two hotdogs and a pretzel from a street cart manned by a very flirty young New Yorker who'd made Jessie blush.

"I'm loving New York so far," Emma said as they walked on.

"I know. Should I say something to Mum soon, do you think? About maybe staying, I mean?"

They crossed the road, dodging a yellow taxi.

"I don't know," Emma said. "I guess you need to wait for the right moment?"

Jessie nodded. "Yeah, you're right. I haven't even asked her about Jack yet."

"You're still sure they're a couple?"

Jessie shook her head. "I'm not sure, but I'd be surprised if they weren't."

"Are you going to ask her?"

Jessie took an enormous bite of her pretzel and gestured at her mouth while she chewed. Once she'd swallowed, she said, "I suppose I'll have to at some point. I doubt she'll tell me unless I ask."

They walked a little further and then Emma said, "Is that the Flatiron building?"

"Yeah," Jessie said and then stopped dead. "Oh wow. Look at the Empire State Building!"

Silhouetted against the sky, it looked smaller than Jessie had been expecting and oddly colourless, like a drawing, but it was still amazing. There'd been a huge photograph of it – probably the world's most famous building – in their old house for as long as Jessie could remember. Black and white and taken from above, so the Empire State was looming out of the surrounding smaller buildings, it was on the landing so you saw it as soon as you started to climb the stairs.

"Dad said that was one of the first things that got him interested in architecture," Jessie told Emma. "I'm going to ring him and tell him we're looking right at it." She fiddled in her pocket for her phone.

Someone almost bumped into the back of them

and Emma glanced over her shoulder, before tugging her friend out of the way.

"We should sit in the park in the shade," Emma said. They headed towards the road just as a man stepped out in front of a car, causing the driver to blare his horn. Emma tugged Jessie towards the zebra crossing.

"When it was built," Jessie said, as they waited for the traffic to slow, "it had a pole on top that was supposed to be for tying hot air balloons to."

Emma looked confused.

"No. Not hot air balloons. Those things like blimps? But that you could travel in?"

"A zeppelin? Like the Hindenberg?" Emma said. They'd learned about the Hindenberg at school. Their history teacher, Mr Baldwin, had been a bit obsessed by it.

"Yes!" Jessie said. "Dad's got a paperweight of the building with a blimp attached. I think mum bought it for him."

"He thinks it was really romantic and exciting. Actually Mum does too – or at least she did. You haven't seen *An Affair to Remember*, have you?"

Emma shook her head.

The old movie was one of her mum's favourites, but Jessie hadn't liked it at all. Why did the woman have to get run over and be permanently disabled when the man got off scot-free? But the idea of meeting the man of your dreams at the Empire State Building definitely appealed.

Jessie and Emma finally managed to cross the road and sat down on a bench in the corner of the park.

"What time is it in England?" Jessie asked, looking at her mobile.

"OK, it's 4 here, so I think it's about 10 there?"

Jessie scrolled to her dad's number and pressed the green button. It only rang a couple of times before she heard her dad's voice and was surprised to find her eyes filling with tears.

"Guess what I'm looking at," she said.

"A box of Krispy Kremes?" he guessed.

Jessie laughed. "Not yet, no. But I'll get one in a minute, since you mentioned it. No. The Empire State Building!"

"Fantastic," John said and Jessie could hear the

smile in his voice. "How's everything?"

"Really good. Are you OK?"

"I'm good. Wishing I was there with you. Hopefully I will be in a couple of weeks."

"What? Really?"

"Yeah. Me and Rhys are hoping to get over for a few days. That OK?"

Jessie grinned into the phone. "That's great."

Working in the Empire State Building hadn't turned out to be quite as interesting as Finn had hoped. The only thing that had kept him going had been the views from the 60th floor windows and he'd only actually been there for a few hours. He'd suspected the job was going to be tedious, but he hadn't quite expected it to be that tedious. He had no idea how he was going to keep it up for the entire summer.

He'd spent the afternoon inputting claims onto a database. Date, name, policy number, details of claim, items lost or damaged. They'd all been depressingly similar. Only a claim for a toilet 'broken by brother-in-law' had stood out.

Walking back uptown, Finn thought about the

conversation he'd had with Sam and Scott on Sunday. He didn't want to stay at his dad's company – if he was honest with himself, he'd known that within minutes of walking in the door and being shown his cubicle. Just the idea of a cubicle made him shudder. But if he didn't work for his dad for the summer, what would he do?

It was all right for Scott, his mom had never put any pressure on him to do anything. Even at school. She just wanted him to be happy and if that meant bumming around and working in a deli then she was fine with that. Or so she said. His dad had left when Scott was seven and now lived on the West Coast with his new family, which was how he'd come to meet Sam: they'd met on a flight back to New York from LA.

But Finn's family was different. They had expectations. Scott had never seemed to understand that. Or at least he didn't understand why Finn went along with it.

At brunch yesterday, Scott and Sam had gone on and on about him trying architecture in some way. But Finn had never thought of architecture as something you tried, he thought of it as a vocation. Something you just did. He'd looked into it in the past. It took, like, seven years. Plus he hadn't taken the preparatory courses he should have. He'd taken drawing and math, obviously, but not pre-calc or physics. And even if he did decide he wanted to change his major, the thought of telling his dad kind of terrified him.

As he crossed 21st Street, he almost walked into the back of two girls who'd stopped dead to look up at the Empire State Building.

"Dad said that was one of the first things that got him interested in architecture," the blonde one said, "I'm going to ring him to tell him we're looking right at it."

Finn almost exclaimed aloud. He glanced at the girls, who were still staring up at New York's most famous landmark and then he looked up at it himself as he continued along Broadway.

Finn didn't really believe in signs...except that he kind of did. It couldn't just be a coincidence that at the very moment he'd been thinking about becoming an architect, and about talking to his dad, that's what he'd overheard.

He was still looking up at the building when he stepped off the kerb and the blare of a taxi horn brought him back to reality and he almost laughed at himself. Yeah, of course it was just a coincidence. A sign. Jesus.

Chapter Ten

Back at Natalie's building, in the lift, Emma tipped her head back and closed her eyes. "That was such a great day. I mean, New York's no Manchester..."

Jessie snorted. "No. If only we'd been at home avoiding the Goths at the bandstand..."

"Trying on sunglasses at Primark..."

"Looking at the floaters in the canal..."

Arriving at Natalie's apartment, Jessie opened the door with the key her mum had given her.

"What are we going to do tonight?" Emma asked as they headed for the living room.

Jessie stopped dead in the doorway.

"Hello, darling!" her mum said, brightly.

Ben was there. Sitting on the sofa. His hair was longer and it suited him like that; curling over his collar and almost, but not quite, hanging over his bright blue eyes. And he was looking at Jessie in the same way he'd looked at her back home: like he knew all her secrets.

"You remember Ben?" Natalie said from her perch on the arm of the sofa. "And Jack?"

Jessie nodded and looked at Jack, who was standing over by the window with his phone in his hand. He was quite good-looking, Jack, but a bit scruffy and sweaty and overweight. You could tell he'd been handsome, like, twenty years ago, but not so much anymore. Like Russell Crowe.

"Ben, did you ever meet Jessie's friend Emma?" Natalie said.

Jessie watched Ben's eyes flick towards Emma. He smiled. "I don't think so, no."

"Hghla," Emma said, before coughing and trying again. "Hello."

"So we've got a business dinner," Natalie said.

Ben stood and stretched, revealing a strip of tanned and toned stomach between the bottom of his T-shirt and the top of his jeans. Jessie felt Emma clutch the back of her T-shirt.

"I've left some cash and a bunch of takeaway menus on the table," Natalie said. "Did you two have a good day?"

"It was great, yeah," Jessie said. "I phoned Dad. He says hello."

"Oh right. Well. Have a good evening. Help yourself to anything you like."

"Will do."

Rounding the silver coffee bean coffee table, Natalie headed for the doorway and Ben and Jack, who was still fiddling with his phone, followed. Jessie stepped out of the way and Emma – still clutching the back of Jessie's T-shirt – moved too.

"See ya," Ben said, as he passed.

The two girls waited until they heard the front door close and then waited a few seconds more, before leaping into the living room, shrieking.

"OH MY GOD!" Emma shrieked. "I mean...OH MY GOD!"

"I told you," Jessie said, throwing herself onto

the sofa, exactly where Ben had been sitting. "Sexy, right?"

"So sexy. My knees went weak. Actually weak. I thought I was going to have to sit on the floor. It's so amazing that he's out here too," Emma said, sighing and fanning herself with her hand.

"Not that amazing," Jessie said. "He's the lead in the play."

"I know. But I'd forgotten. And then there he was."

Jessie smiled. Yes. There he was.

She'd first met him at the rehearsals for her mum's play in a studio in Castlefield. The room was a long rectangle with a big window at one end and mirrors all down one side. Jessie was sitting on a really uncomfortable stool, fidgeting and fiddling. She was actually wondering if she could get away with slipping her headphones on. She was bored.

But then she noticed Ben looking at her in the mirror. He was sitting on the same side of the room as her so it would have been obvious if he'd been looking at her straight on, but he could see her in the mirror while looking straight ahead. She'd looked away. But when she looked back he was still looking. He had a little smile on his face and after a couple of minutes, Jessie wondered if she had something on her face or if her trousers were undone or she'd ripped her top or something. She tried to check herself out without making it obvious and she couldn't see anything. She looked back. He was still looking at her. Natalie was talking about the play. What it meant. What her inspiration had been. What she wanted from the actors. She'd been talking for a while. And the entire time, Ben had been looking at her. At Jessie. The entire time.

She was sure something would have happened with him if her mum's play hadn't taken off and he hadn't left. But he was there. In New York. Maybe she'd get a second chance.

Finn stopped off at Aroma to pick up a couple of coffees and then got the lift up to his family's apartment. He'd come to love the building as much as his parents did. It was a former hotel and pretty amazing inside and out. Plus it was full of history. It was once the 'Grandest Hotel in Manhattan' and tons of celebrities had stayed there.

Finn opened the door and called out, "Anybody home?"

"In here, darling," his mom called. He found her in the kitchen, sitting in the vintage diner booth his parents had had installed.

She looked up at him over her glasses, which had slid down to the end of her nose.

"How'd it go?"

Finn kissed her, sat down opposite and put the iced latte he'd bought on the table in front of her.

"It was OK," he said.

Diane sighed. "Only OK?"

"Yeah. It was... The stuff I had to do? It wasn't all that interesting."

She took her glasses off and put them down on top of the book. "Well it was only the first day. As you get used to it, you'll get more responsibility and you'll start to learn more..."

"The thing is," Finn said and then paused to gulp some of his drink. "The thing is, I'm not sure I want to learn more."

Diane chewed her bottom lip, the way she always did when she wasn't sure about what she was going to say. "It's important to your father," she said eventually.

"I know," Finn said. "But it shouldn't be, should it? I mean, it's his job and he loves it and he wants to share it with me – I get that – but I'm not interested in insurance. I'm just not."

"You can't say that yet though, can you? You don't know enough about it. You remember when you didn't want to play soccer? You said you weren't interested and you ended up loving it."

"I was five, Mom! I'm going to be 18 soon – I think I know—"

"Oh!" Diane interrupted. "I need to talk to you about that."

"About what?"

"About you being 18."

"No," Finn said, knowing exactly what she was about to say.

"Oh Finn. You know it would mean so much to her."

"No."

"Just a small party."

"No."

"You see, the thing is..."

"Aw jeez, she's already arranged it?!" Finn ran his hands through his hair.

"Yes. She wanted it to be a surprise party, but I knew I'd better warn you..."

Finn groaned.

"It'll make her happy."

"Great. So I'm working at Consolidated to make Dad happy and having a surprise party to make Gran happy. What about me? When do I get to be happy?"

His mom laughed. "When you're grown and you've got kids of your own to torment." She put her glasses back on and picked up her book.

"Thank you," Finn said, smiling in spite of himself. "Thanks a lot."

Chapter Eleven

"So what are you up to today?" Natalie asked over coffee and toast.

"No plans," Jessie said, looking at Emma for confirmation. "We're just going to wander and see where it takes us."

"That's a good way to get to know New York," Natalie said. "But remember that if you go anywhere and feel threatened or uncomfortable, get out of there. Trust your intuition."

"We will. We'll probably stick to busy areas anyway."

"I want to go to Macy's," Emma said.

Natalie laughed. "Oh well, I don't think you'll feel

threatened in Macy's. I could live in Macy's."

"What are you working on today?" Emma asked.

"Oh, the new play," Natalie said, waving her hand as if it was no big deal.

"What's it about?" Jessie asked.

Natalie frowned and immediately put one finger to the bridge of her nose, as if to smooth out the little groove that had appeared. "I'm not entirely sure yet. Relationships, mainly." She smiled. "Same as everything ever written."

She drained her coffee and stood up. "Let me know when you go, OK?"

Once Jessie and Emma had finished their breakfast, they grabbed their bags and Jessie knocked on Natalie's office door, pushing it open.

"We're off," she said.

Natalie swung around in her chair, smiling. "Have a great day. If you do get to Macy's, could you pick me up an eyebrow pencil? Fling by MAC?"

"No probs. Have a good... Good writing, I mean. Enjoy your writing."

"I will, sweetie," Natalie said and swung back to her desk. Jessie closed the door.

"I just told my mum to 'have a good writing'," she told Emma, wincing. "Why am I such an idiot around her?"

Emma laughed. "You're not. Most of the time."

They let themselves out of the apartment and got in the lift.

"I just wish I could be completely relaxed with her, you know? Like I am with dad."

"But weren't things a bit funny with your dad when he first told you about Rhys?" Emma said. "I remember you saying then that you didn't really know what to say to him."

"Yeah. You're right. I'd forgotten about that."

"And everything's fine with him now, right?"

"Yeah. I miss him, actually. I didn't think I would, but I do."

"You just need time to adjust to being around your mum again. It's been a while since you've spent so much time with her, you just need to get used to each other again, I think."

"Yeah. It's just—" They got out of the lift. "It's just that even you seem more relaxed with her than I am."

Emma pushed open the building's heavy door and, as it had done every day so far, the heat hit them, making them gasp.

"Are you sure we should walk?" Emma asked.

"We'll miss stuff if we don't. We'll get something to drink and go in lots of air-conditioned shops. We'll be fine."

They started walking down Broadway and then Emma said, "It's easier for me to be more relaxed with her. Your mum. I don't have the same issues with her as you do, so you shouldn't compare it – you're being tough on yourself."

"I know," Jessie said. They crossed at the crossing and then again so they could walk through Verdi Square. "It's just hard."

"Well you know what my dad says," Emma said, smiling. "Life's hard."

Jessie laughed. "Yeah. And then you die."

The park was teeming with people, walking their dogs, feeding the birds or just sitting with their faces turned up to the sun.

"This used to be a no-go area, apparently," Emma said. "I was reading about it in the guide book. They called it Needle Park. I think it got closed down for a while."

"Really?" Jessie said. "You wouldn't know it, would you? It's so gorgeous now."

Emma stumbled and said, "Oh crap."

"What?"

"I fell off my flip-flop. Ow."

"Do you want to go back and change?"

"No, I'm OK, thanks. Just clumsy." She stood on one leg and pulled her shoe back on. "They're actually a lot comfier than they look."

Coming out of the park, they crossed two more streets to take them to Gray's Papaya.

"They go here in *You've Got Mail*, you know?" Jessie said as they waited to be served. "And I think they sit over by the park too."

"Cool," Emma said. "I'm starting to wish I hadn't had toast now. They do donuts."

"You can get a donut another day. What juice are you getting?"

Jessie got Papaya Juice and Emma ordered a non-alcoholic Banana Daiquiri.

"I can't believe you got a banana drink," Jessie

said as they left. "We need something refreshing. There's nothing refreshing about a banana." Jessie looked around, trying to work out which way to head.

"Do we get to Central Park if we walk down here?" Emma asked, pointing down 72nd Street.

Jessie squinted. "I think so, yeah."

"Let's go that way then. We've kind of done this bit of Broadway."

Jessie grinned. "Jaded already..."

"Ha! Hardly. But there's nothing much to see down that way. Not for a while anyway. I thought we were supposed to be getting lost and finding new places today."

Halfway down the block, they realised it was the same way they'd walked with Natalie.

"We're crap at getting lost, obviously," Emma said.

"Yep. If we keep going along here, it takes us to the Dakota, remember?"

"So shall we go down here instead?"

They walked down what turned out to be Columbus Avenue.

"This is much nicer than Broadway," Jessie said after a couple of blocks, and then she squealed.

"And there's the Magnolia Bakery!"

They peered through the window and Emma said, "I'm still regretting that toast."

"If you hadn't had the toast, you would've had a donut so you still wouldn't be getting a cupcake. If it's still open when we come home, we can get one then." She looked at the opening times in the window. "It doesn't close until 10. We've got plenty of time."

"I know. But they look so delicious. And Carrie and Miranda sat here on a bench." She looked around. "There's no bench."

"Maybe that was a different branch. Or they put the bench in just for the show."

"Crap. I was going to sit on it. These stupid flip-flops are bloody killing me." She leaned on Jessie, lifted one foot and pulled one of her shoes off. "Thank God. I thought it was embedded."

"We'll go back and you can find something more sensible to wear," Jessie said.

"I would usually take the piss out of the sensible shoes thing, but this time I think you're right. Do we have to walk though?" Emma put her foot back down, wincing.

Jessie smiled. "No. We can get a cab."

They managed to flag down a cab and climbed in. It turned off Columbus and took them down a gorgeous tree-lined street, past apartments that looked very much like Carrie Bradshaw's, before heading back up Broadway and depositing them outside the Albright.

Emma hobbled to the door, whimpering. "Sitting down made it feel so much worse."

"Well I'm not carrying you to the apartment," Jessie said.

They got the lift and let themselves in. Jessie called out that they were back, but didn't bother knocking on Natalie's door – they weren't going to be long, there was no point in breaking her concentration.

Emma changed into trainers and socks. "Not stylish, but at least I can walk."

Jessie waved her hand, "All New York women wear trainers – haven't you seen *Working Girl*?"

"No," Emma said. "I haven't. I haven't seen half the New York films you've seen."

"We should watch some. I bet Mum's got them on DVD somewhere."

Jessie called out 'bye' as they let themselves out again and waited for the lift. The lift doors opened and Ben was standing inside, looking completely startled.

"Ben!" Jessie said, without thinking.

"Hi," he said.

The lift doors started to close and he put his foot in and then stepped out onto the landing.

"Hi," he said, again.

"Are you here to see Mum?" Jessie asked.

Ben looked around. He looked nervous.

"Ah. No," he said. He ran a hand through his hair. "No. I, ah, thought you two might want someone to show you around New York."

"Really?" Emma said. "That would be fantastic. Thank you!"

"So you're ready to go then?" he said.

Jessie laughed. "Yes! You almost missed us. Actually you did miss us. We've been out once, but Emma's shoes were hurting so we came back. You should've phoned!"

The three of them got in the lift.

"Yeah, sorry," Ben said. "I was up here anyway

so I just thought I'd call in."

"Oh no, no need to apologise," Emma said. "This is great. Thank you."

"So what were you up here for?" Jessie asked, looking straight ahead. She was worried that if she looked directly at him, she'd be too nervous to speak to him. "Where do you live?"

"Not too far away," he said. "About ten blocks? My bank's up here."

"Cool," Jessie said.

They followed Ben out onto the street and started walking the same way Jessie and Emma had already walked and Emma repeated her Needle Park information to Ben.

"So where were you thinking of taking us?" Emma asked him, as they crossed the road, passed Gray's Papaya, and headed down 72nd Street. Again.

"Er. The park?" Ben said.

Jessie and Emma looked at each other.

"That's great," Jessie said. "But we've been to the park a couple of times already..."

"Oh, right," Ben said. "Yeah, of course. Have you been to the Boathouse Café?"

Jessie nodded. "Yeah, Mum took us."

"What about the zoo?"

Jessie and Emma looked at each other again. Emma pulled a confused face.

"Central Park Zoo?" Jessie asked. "No, we haven't yet. Is it good?"

Ben nodded. "It's really good, yeah."

They crossed Columbus and continued towards the Dakota.

"Did my mum ask you to do this?" Jessie asked. "Show us around, I mean."

Ben laughed. "No. Not at all, no. I just thought it would be good. You know, I didn't know anyone when I moved here, so..."

"It's really nice of you," Jessie said. "The zoo sounds great."

They walked into the park and Emma and Jessie asked Ben about moving to New York and the play and how much his life had changed. He wasn't exactly chatty, but he certainly talked more than Jessie had ever heard him talk before. He seemed shy, which surprised her, but it probably shouldn't have done. A lot of actors claimed to be shy, didn't they. It made her like him even more. When she'd first met him, she'd thought he was a bit cocky, but now he seemed almost vulnerable. Just walking along next to him, she had butterflies and she could feel that her hands were shaking. It reminded her of the first couple of times she went out with Taylor. Which made her feel a bit sick. She told herself to calm down.

Ben paid their entrance into the zoo – even though they offered to pay for themselves – and then he excused himself to go to the loo.

"So," Emma said, as soon as he'd gone. "WTAF?"

"I know!" Jessie said. "It's weird, right? And he seems nervous?"

"He likes you. Obviously. That's why he turned up, that's why he's nervous."

Jessie grinned. "Do you think?"

"What else could it be?"

"Maybe he's just being nice? Maybe Mum really did ask him to do this, but told him not to say?"

"But then why would he be so nervous? No. I think he likes you. He's probably been waiting all this time for you to come and visit. Counting the days until he saw you again!" Emma grinned.

"Yeah, right. But the zoo? I mean...you take kids to the zoo."

"Oh I think the zoo's a great place for a first date!"

Jessie pulled a face. "This is not a first date!"

"Well, no. Cos I'm here. Ooh! Do you want me to wander off and leave the two of you alone?"

"God, no. No, I need you. Don't leave me. I wouldn't know what to say to him."

"That doesn't bode well for your future relationship," Emma said, grinning.

"Shut up. Now, I mean. When he comes back, you do the talking. My mind keeps going blank."

"Right. So I'm like a court jester or something," Emma said, smiling. "And a gooseberry. Lucky me."

Finn walked down the tree-lined avenue leading to the zoo. He stopped and looked up at the clock over the entrance. It had brass animals that came out and chimed the hour, but he'd just missed them. Still, it meant he'd made good time, he didn't need to be there until 11.15. Should he go in or wait outside? He and Scott had just said they'd meet at the zoo, they just hadn't said where exactly.

He sat down on a park bench and texted Scott to tell him he'd arrived. He looked at the clock tower again. He used to come here every Saturday morning with his gran. Not to the zoo, although Gran was a 'friend of the zoo' with a lifetime unlimited membership, but to the park. Even if they weren't going to see the animals, Finn still insisted they pass this way, so he could look at the clock tower. And then they'd go to the Carousel or to Sheep Meadow or the Reservoir. The trips almost always ended with brunch at the Boathouse Cafe and then, once he was a teenager, lunch at the Inn on the Park.

He couldn't remember the last time they'd done it. He wasn't even sure why they'd stopped.

"Hey, man."

Finn looked up to see Scott loping towards him. Scott tipped his head, draining the last of a Starbucks, and then threw the cup in a nearby trash can.

"Sam said to call her when we got here and she'll let us in," Scott said. He pulled his cell out of his pocket.

Finn stood and the two of them walked towards the main entrance, while Scott talked to Sam. All he said was, "Hey, babe. We're outside," but Finn's stomach still clenched with jealousy. To be able to just call her like that, not to even have to introduce himself. To have already made the arrangements at some other time. Maybe over dinner. Maybe in bed. Finn looked at Scott. He wondered if he knew how lucky he was.

"I can't believe she's working here," Scott said. "Of all the cool places in the city..."

"Oh yeah," Finn said. "So...have you taken Valium or something? I don't want to have to carry you out of here."

Scott pulled a face. "I'm not scared!"

Finn grinned.

"I'm not! I just don't see why anyone would want to come here when they could go to, like, the Guggenheim."

"When did *you* last go to The Guggenheim?"

"Yeah, OK, not necessarily The Guggenheim, but, you know, wherever. The Met. The Mets, even. Anywhere."

"I think you're missing the point of zoos. There are no penguins at The Met."

Scott pulled a face and shrugged as if the idea of people paying to see penguins was a ridiculous one.

"And yet, here you are," Finn said.

"I'm here to see Sam, not the animals," he grinned. "Sam in her natural habitat."

"She's liking it then? The internship?"

"She loves it. She's already talking about changing her major."

"Really?" Finn said, but he didn't get to ask anything else, because then Sam was there, opening the gate and grinning at the two of them.

She kissed Scott and kind of squeezed Finn's arm. She was wearing the zoo uniform of an olive green polo shirt and knee-length tan shorts, which weren't exactly a flattering combination, but she still looked gorgeous. "So," she said. "Seal feeding is in about ten minutes, so we'll walk over there?"

Scott rolled his eyes. "I must really love you," he said and Finn considered making some excuse and just leaving. He wasn't sure if he could stand to be a third wheel for the rest of the morning.

***

When Ben came out of the loos, he seemed a bit less nervous.

"Maybe he just really needed a wee," Emma whispered to Jessie.

"Maybe he's taken something," Jessie whispered back. "He needs to be drugged to get through the day with me."

"That's the spirit!" Emma said, rolling her eyes.

Ben led them straight over to a board on which the day's activities and events were listed.

"There's seal feeding in about ten minutes," he said. "What do you think?"

"Sounds good," Jessie said.

They walked over to the seals and found a good position against the railings, opposite the big rock that Ben said the seals hopped up on to do tricks.

"Do you come here a lot?" Jessie asked, still wondering why he'd picked the zoo of all places.

"No. I've been a couple of times," Ben said. "I've been with, ah, friends and I brought my mum when she came over to see me."

"I bet she misses you," Emma said. "Your mum."

Ben smiled. "Yeah, she does. She's really great, though. My dad – they're divorced – he didn't think coming out here was a good idea but Mum told me to go for it."

"So what did she think of the play?" Jessie asked him.

Ben turned to look at her and his face had lit up. Jessie almost gasped – he was so gorgeous.

"She really loved it," he said. "She'd seen it loads of times back in Manchester, obviously, but to be able to bring her to Broadway...she was really proud."

"I bet," Jessie said.

"But you must be really proud of your mum too," he said.

Jessie looked out at the seals, who obviously knew feeding time was approaching because they'd all started getting closer to the big rock.

"I am, yeah," she said. "And I'm looking forward to seeing the play again."

"You saw it in Manchester, right?" Ben asked.

Jessie nodded. "Yeah. And I was at the rehearsals."

"Were you? At Castlefield?"

"A few times, yeah," Jessie said. She couldn't

believe he didn't remember. She'd been sure he'd been staring at her. He *had* been staring at her, hadn't he? How could he not remember?

She watched as the trainer let himself in to the seal enclosure, carrying two buckets of fish and spent the next fifteen minutes watching the seals do various tricks to earn them. The animals jumped and clapped and even climbed up onto the rock and waved at the crowd. It was really cute, but Jessie spent the whole time wondering if she'd misinterpreted Ben's interest in her. But the fact was, he'd come to the apartment to take them out today. He wouldn't have done that if he didn't have any interest in her at all, would he? Unless he thought she'd be a good summer fling or something. But then that would be a bit risky given that he was performing in her mum's play. Presumably he wouldn't want to risk upsetting her mum.

By the time the seal trainer left the enclosure, Jessie wanted to bang her head on the railings just to stop the constant chatter in her brain.

The seal feeding was very cool and took Finn's mind off Scott and Sam...mostly. He couldn't resist sneaking glances at them every now and then. He was so envious of Scott's easy affection with her. It was fair enough, since Sam was his girlfriend, but just the fact that he could drape his arm around her shoulders, stroke her hair, hold her hand...it seemed incredible to Finn.

And he also felt guilty. Scott was his best friend. He was happy. Finn should be happy for him. Shouldn't he? He knew that wanting his best friend's girlfriend wasn't healthy. It wasn't good for Finn, since he knew nothing was ever going to happen, and it wasn't good for his relationship with Scott since he didn't want to resent him. He loved him. They'd known each other for years. But even knowing it wasn't healthy and it was pointless couldn't seem to make a difference. He couldn't stop liking Sam. He wished he could.

As the seal trainer left the enclosure, Sam turned and put her hand on Finn's arm and he actually flinched his arm away. Sam looked a bit startled, but took it in her stride and set off leading them to the next thing she wanted them to see. Finn followed, feeling like a complete idiot.

***

Once the seals had finished their performance, Jessie, Emma and Ben walked around the rest of the zoo. Ben wasn't exactly chatty, but he definitely seemed more relaxed in their company than he'd been at the beginning. As they headed to the exit, Ben said, "I'm going to have to get going. I need to, you know, get ready for the show this afternoon."

"Oh right, yeah, of course," Jessie said. She felt disappointed, but also a tiny bit relieved. It was so tiring having to keep on your toes to avoid saying or doing something completely humiliating in front of a boy you liked.

"It must be hard, working every day," Emma said.

Ben nodded. "Well, I get two nights off – I'm off tonight – but yeah. Especially here. There's so much cool stuff to do at night. Actually there's a film on in Bryant Park tonight. You know, on an outdoor screen. It's pretty cool."

"Are you going?" Emma asked him.

"No," he said. "I'm having dinner with a friend, but you guys should go. People take picnics and it gets really busy. I don't know what film's on though."

"That sounds great," Jessie said. "Thanks."

Once they were out of the zoo, they started walking towards the nearest park exit and then Ben said, "I'm going to have to leg it. Sorry. It's been really good, yeah?"

"Yes," Jessie said. "Thanks so much."

"See you again," he said. And then practically broke into a run.

"Well," Jessie said, once he was out of earshot. "He couldn't get away from me quick enough, could he?"

"Oh come on!" Emma said, laughing. "It's not like he made up some excuse! He's got the show!"

"Yeah, in, like, six hours or something."

"He probably needs to prepare, darling," Emma said, in a dramatic voice. "And he said 'See you again'."

"Yeah. He meant both of us. And he didn't ask for my number. And, may I remind you, he *ran* away."

Emma shrugged. "I'm not buying it. I think he likes you. And you like him."

"I do," Jessie agreed. "I think."

***

Once the seals had finished their performance, Sam showed Finn and Scott around the rest of the zoo and told them what she'd done so far. She was being given the opportunity to try everything, from shovelling up after the animals to entertaining children in the education centre.

"It sounds like a really great internship," Finn said, as they arrived back at the main exit.

"It is," Sam said. "I'm really loving it. And the penguins are great."

She grinned as Scott shuddered. He'd actually refused to go inside to see the penguins from the underwater viewing area so Sam and Finn had gone without him. As they'd watched the birds swimming up to the glass and then swooping away, Finn had stood next to Sam and pretended she was his girlfriend and they were on a date, alone.

After about five minutes, Sam nudged her body against him and said, "We'd better go."

He followed her out, wishing instead that he could have pressed her up against the glass and kissed her.

And now they were saying goodbye and Scott was kissing Sam while Finn stared past them, out into the park.

"Hey, listen," Sam said, when she and Scott had finished. "There's a movie in Bryant Park tonight – do you fancy it?"

"What is it?" Scott asked.

"Not sure, but it's usually something good, isn't it? We could get a picnic. What do you think, Finn?"

"Oh, I don't know," Finn said. He thought he'd probably had enough of watching Scott and Sam kiss for one day.

"Come on," Scott said. "What else you gonna do? I'm gonna go down to work now anyway so I can bring some food from there."

"Oh come on, Finn!" Sam said. "It'll be fun."

Finn frowned. What else was he going to do? And at least he'd get to spend the evening with Sam. And Scott. His best friend, Scott.

"I'll see you both there," he said.

Chapter Twelve

Bryant Park was already fairly busy by the time Jessie and Emma arrived. People had laid out picnic blankets or set out folding chairs. Some people had umbrellas up, to shelter them from the sun. The whole place was buzzing.

Jessie and Emma found a spot as close to the middle as they could. They wanted to be able to see the screen, but also soak up the atmosphere.

"This already feels like a proper New York experience," Emma said, as they arranged their shopping bags at their feet where they could see them.

"The whole day's been a proper New York experience," Jessie said.

Once they'd left the Zoo, they'd walked down Fifth Avenue and spent the afternoon in and out of all of the iconic shops they'd known about for years. They'd tried on shoes in Saks and make-up in Macy's. Jessie had even remembered to buy her mum the eyebrow pencil from MAC.

She'd also rung her mum to see if she wanted to join them for the film, but Natalie had said she was going out for dinner with a friend. Instead, Jessie's mum ordered a picnic for them – they just had to collect it from a kiosk in the park.

"I'll go and get the picnic," Emma said. "Before it gets too busy."

Emma left and Jessie leaned back on her hands and looked around. She couldn't quite believe she was really there. In New York. At an outdoor movie.

The park was surrounded by skyscrapers. Directly in front of her was an enormous modern glass building reflecting the older buildings on the opposite side of the park – she got out her phone and took a photo. She could see the Empire State Building too. It made her miss her dad. Could she really leave him in Manchester and move to New

York? Could she really live with her mum? If her mum even wanted her to... She wasn't sure. The whole prospect was kind of terrifying.

But when she thought about going back to Manchester, back to the same school, up to Sixth Form, on to university...it made her heart sink. It didn't feel scary, but it didn't feel right either. New York felt right. For a few years now she'd been worrying because, unlike most of her friends, she had no idea what she wanted to do with her life. But now she thought maybe she'd been worrying about the wrong thing. She should have been thinking not about what she wanted to do, but *where* she wanted to do it. She felt now that if she moved to New York, everything might just fall in to place.

By the time Emma got back with the picnic, Jessie had pretty much convinced herself that she moving to New York was the right decision. Now all she needed to do was convince her parents.

While his bag was being inspected, Finn looked around for Scott and Sam. The park was ridiculously busy, crammed with people. Unless Scott and Sam had already secured a spot on the lawn, they were going to have to sit on the surrounding gravel.

He started walking around the perimeter of the park, but couldn't see them, so he sat down on a low wall and texted Scott.

While he waited for his reply, he looked around. He really did love this kind of New York experience. There was a great atmosphere, everyone was talking and laughing and the sun had started to go down so the weather was cooling too.

His phone buzzed in his hand and he read Scott's message: 'Sorry. Stuck @ work. Sam is there. Txt her. Sorry.'

Finn stared at the message. He didn't know whether he was disappointed or pleased. Or terrified. If he'd been worried about spending the evening as a third wheel, he was possibly even more worried about spending an evening alone with Sam in such a romantic situation. And what was Scott playing at? Why was he stuck at work again? The deli was supposed to be a casual, part-time job. Why didn't he just leave?

Finn wondered again if Scott was cheating on

Sam. And if he was, then he was treating Finn like a complete idiot too. What was he thinking? That it wasn't a problem standing Sam up because Finn would be there to take care of her? Old reliable Finn. Like Finn posed no threat to Scott and Sam's relationship at all?

Finn's cell buzzed again. 'I can see you!' it said.

It was from Sam. Almost immediately, hands covered his eyes and he heard Sam say, "Guess who?"

He felt his stomach flip. This was such a bad idea.

By the time the film started, Jessie and Emma had eaten almost all of their completely delicious picnic – mozzarella and tomato sandwiches, potato salad and frittata – and the park was absolutely crammed with people.

The film was *The Goodbye Girl*. Neither Jessie nor Emma had seen it before, but it was set in New York and they loved trying to spot places that they'd already seen or been.

The crowd didn't watch quietly like in a cinema, but shouted encouragement and abuse at the characters. And when the main character got mugged and her flatmate chased the muggers through the streets, Jessie and Emma yelled and screamed along with everyone else.

But Jessie found she couldn't entirely concentrate on the film. Instead she was thinking about what she would say to her dad. Fortunately, he and Rhys were now coming to New York the following weekend, for a short break and to see Jessie, so maybe she'd get a chance to suggest her plan then. But she just wasn't sure whether she should talk to her mum first. She probably should, since she'd be the one Jessie would be living with. But she also felt as if she'd be going behind her dad's back. She thought she should at least run it past him and see how he felt about it before making any arrangements with Natalie.

She just wasn't sure what she should do for the best.

Finn had been right, he and Sam had ended up sitting on the gravel, on chairs borrowed from the outdoor cafes, but he'd really enjoyed himself anyway.

Sam had talked a lot during the movie and because the park was so noisy, that had meant her putting her mouth right up to his ear, her hair tickling his face. She'd touched him a lot too. On his arm, on his knee. After Finn had gone and bought pizza slices for the two of them – they had no food without Scott to bring it – she'd even wiped a bit of tomato sauce off his cheek with her thumb.

He couldn't think straight. He wanted her. But she was his best friend's girlfriend. But Scott wasn't there. Scott was working. Or screwing around. Either way, he wasn't there and Finn was. And he thought maybe Sam liked him. She hadn't even seemed that disappointed when Finn had told her Scott wasn't coming. She'd just grinned at him and hopped over the wall to sit next to him. Then, when they'd gone to find the seats, she'd linked her arm through his. Maybe she was as conflicted as Finn was?

The film finished and they quickly headed out of the park, before the rush. As they walked down Sixth, Sam said, "Do you want to go and get a drink or something?"

Finn looked at her. He probably shouldn't. He had

work in the morning, he had to be up. And he also wasn't sure he should be spending any more time alone with her. So he forced himself to say no and flagged down a cab. As it pulled away, she blew him a kiss and he laughed out loud.

Or something... he thought to himself, as he started walking back up Sixth towards home.

Chapter Thirteen

Jessie and Emma spent the following week investigating New York while Natalie wrote and let them get on with it.

They did all the things Jessie had daydreamed about doing. They went to Grand Central Station and whispered smut to each other via the Whispering Walls until they were both helpless with laughter. They fed the pigeons outside the Plaza Hotel and they spent one day lounging in Central Park in the sunshine and another day getting the Staten Island Ferry over to the Statue of Liberty. Jessie had tried to convince Emma to go up the Empire State Building with her, but Emma wasn't a fan of heights and wouldn't be convinced.

Natalie occasionally emerged from her office to take them out to dinner or eat takeaways with them.

They didn't hear anything from Ben.

But Emma wasn't worried.

"He's really busy, I bet," she told Jessie as they sat in the Apple Store emailing their friends for free. "Particularly during the week."

Jessie rolled her eyes. "I don't know," she said. "I think I was just kidding myself. He was just being nice."

"I really thought he liked you," Emma said. She swung her stool around to face Jessie.

Jessie smiled. "I hoped he did. But it's OK. He took my mind off Taylor and that's the main thing."

"True," Emma said.

"Although is it healthier that I'm now obsessing over Ben instead of obsessing over Taylor?"

Emma smiled. "You've hardly been obsessing."

"I don't know. I've thought about him a lot. But it's OK. It wouldn't make sense anyway, really. If I don't get to come here next year."

"You're really serious about moving here?"

Emma said. "It's so exciting."

Jessie swung the monitor in front of her so Emma could see the screen. She was on the website for Columbia University School of the Arts.

"Wow," Emma said.

"I know," Jessie said, smiling. She clicked on a link to Theatre Arts. "I thought maybe I could start with this. See if some of mum's, you know, whatever it is has rubbed off on me."

"I think that's a great idea," Emma said. "But I'm not sure you've thought it through. What the hell am I going to do without you?"

Jessie laughed. "Well nothing's decided yet. I haven't even spoken to my mum. Or Dad."

"But he's coming this weekend, isn't he?"

"Sunday. They're staying for the week. Dad's got some meetings."

"So you're going to talk to them then? And your mum?"

"I think so. I'll just have to see how it goes."

On Saturday night they went to see Natalie's play, *Small Change*.

Jessie had been looking forward to seeing it, although she never would have admitted it to her mum. She'd seen it in its earliest rehearsals – in that Manchester studio where she first met Ben – and she'd seen it in Manchester and then when it transferred to London. She still couldn't quite believe it was on Broadway. So many of Jessie's favourite actors and actresses of all time had appeared on Broadway and she couldn't quite believe her own mother had written a play that was such a massive hit there.

Natalie seemed quite giddy at the prospect of taking them to her show. She was ready to go before the girls and had switched off her computer for once. She waited for them at the kitchen table, flicking nervously through *The New York Times*.

The three of them were soon all in a taxi, being driven down Broadway, Jessie felt her mum squeeze her arm and turned to look at her. Natalie gave a nervous smile and Jessie smiled back. She hadn't really stopped to think of what her mum had achieved. A successful play on Broadway was a big deal. She *should* be really proud. But it was hard because she didn't feel like she was part of Natalie's success at all. She'd been in the rehearsal studio right at the beginning, but then once it had all taken off, Jessie had been left to her own boring life and her mum had shot off ahead without her. Natalie never even seemed to look back.

Eventually they turned off Broadway and the taxi driver pulled up.

"Here we are!" Natalie sang.

Getting out of the cab, Jessie looked up and felt a pang of disappointment. The building was really dull. Brown brick with metal fire escapes running along the front. There was a canopy with the show's name – SMALL CHANGE – on it, but it wasn't lit up. And they weren't even on Broadway.

"What street is this?" Jessie asked, when her mum joined her outside the theatre.

"44th." Natalie turned and beamed up at the theatre.

"I thought your play was on Broadway," Jessie said.

Her mum gave a little laugh. "Oh, Broadway just means the theatre district, the theatre doesn't actually have to be *on* Broadway itself."

"Oh," Jessie said. She hadn't known that. She probably should have known that.

"Let's go in and I'll show you around," Natalie said.

Jessie and Emma followed her into the lobby, where she greeted everyone she passed. She led them backstage and Jessie started to feel excited again. She was backstage at a Broadway theatre!

"Mum," she said. "Did anyone I like ever appear here?"

"I think Harry Potter did a show here," Natalie said, distractedly. "I don't mean Harry Potter, do I? The actor. Daniel Radcliffe."

"Mum!" Jessie said, rolling her eyes at Emma who, she could tell, was remembering that Daniel Radcliffe was naked in that play. Emma had gone a bit glassy-eyed at the thought. "Someone I like. You know, Audrey Hepburn? Doris Day? Someone like that."

"Oh right, yes. Er. I think Audrey Hepburn did do a play here, now that you mention it. I think I remember reading that."

Jessie felt butterflies start in her stomach.

Audrey Hepburn had performed here? She grinned at Emma, who grinned back.

"Oh wait," Natalie said, stopping. "Or was it Katharine Hepburn?"

Jessie rolled her eyes. She liked Katharine Hepburn too, but not as much as Audrey. And knowing her mum, it was neither of them.

Natalie knocked on a nearby door and then pushed it open and walked in before stopping dead, almost causing Jessie and Emma to bump into her.

The two girls peeped around her and saw Ben, sitting in a chair, wearing just his underpants. Slightly too baggy underpants, Jessie noticed, before Natalie said, "Oh! Sorry!" and shuffled them back out of the room.

"We'll come and see Ben in a little while," Natalie said. She'd gone a bit pink. "Let's see who else is around."

Jessie and Emma followed her down the hallway, Natalie still smiling and chatting and schmoozing as she went.

"It's like being out with the Queen or something," Jessie mumbled.

"Oh! Here's Jack!" Natalie said and Jessie rolled her eyes. Jack. Of course.

"Hello again," Jack said, smiling at Jessie and Emma.

They both smiled back politely.

"You've come to see your mum's show then?" he asked and slung his arm casually around Natalie's shoulder. Jessie bristled, but Natalie looked completely comfortable.

"Actually is there a loo?" Jessie said. "I really need the loo."

"What was that about?" Emma asked in the bathroom.

"I can't bear him being all friendly and charming with his arm around my mum. Why can't they just admit they're a couple?"

"Oh I don't know," Emma said, between lip-gloss applications. "Maybe because you make him feel about as welcome as a..." She scrunched up her eyes in thought.

"Something not very welcome?" Jessie guessed, trying not to smile.

"...your period when you're wearing white jeans!" Emma said triumphantly.

"Ew," Jessie said. "And when have you ever worn white jeans?"

"I wouldn't would I. For that reason. So what's your problem with him though, really?"

"What apart from how he's a home-wrecker?"

Emma raised one eyebrow.

"Yeah, I know. But he kind of is. That's where it started."

"You don't think your parents splitting up had more to do with, oh, I don't know, your dad being gay?"

"Yeah, but that's something else. I coped with that, didn't I? I didn't freak. So why won't she just tell me about her and Jack? Especially when it's so obvious!"

"I don't think it's obvious," Emma said.

"Are you joking?! He's all over her!"

"He just put his arm around her. Didn't Gareth ever put his arm around you?"

At the thought of Gareth, the creepy bloke Jessie used to work with at the local leisure centre, Jessie and Emma both shuddered.

"Never say anything like that again," Jessie said, holding up a warning finger.

"I won't. Sorry. I even made myself feel a bit sick."

They found Jessie's mum and Jack sitting very close together and chatting quietly. Jessie gave Emma a look to say, "See!"

While they were waiting for Natalie to finish her conversation, Jessie spotted Ben emerging from his dressing room and elbowed Emma. As he walked down the corridor towards them, Jessie felt her stomach flipping over. He was so gorgeous – he was dressed now of course – and he was staring straight at her. It was only when he stopped in front of them that she realised she'd been staring straight at him too. With her mouth hanging open and, no doubt, an utterly gormless expression on her face. Great.

"Hey," he said. "Sorry about before." He jerked his head back to indicate his dressing room.

"That's OK," Jessie said, "It was...h-erm...fine."

"So you're going to be watching the show then?" Ben asked.

Jessie nodded.

"And are you coming to the after-party?"

"I think so, yeah," Jessie said. Her mum hadn't even mentioned an after-party, but if there was one, Jessie was going to insist on going.

"See you there then," Ben said and left.

Jessie and Emma watched him go. "Were you going to say 'hot'?" Emma asked eventually.

"Yes!" Jessie said. She wanted to cry. "Oh my God! The shame!"

"I think you got away with it," Emma said. But then she ruined it by snorting with laughter.

The theatre auditorium was as uninspiring as the exterior. The seats were a garish purple and the decor was nowhere near as fancy as the London theatre, although they were sitting in a box, which was pretty cool and had a chandelier, at least.

"This is so cool!" Emma said, squeezing Jessie's arm.

And it was cool – Jessie knew it was. But it was also surreal. She couldn't quite get her head around the fact that this was her mum's play. This was her mum's life. And it was so different from her own.

Next to Jessie, her mum was distracted, fiddling

with her phone and craning her head to scan the auditorium, but then the lights went down and she sat back in her seat. She gave Jessie a brief smile and then Jessie sat back too.

And they watched the play.

Chapter Fourteen

As the cab pulled up outside The Campbell Hotel, Finn's stomach lurched. He paid the driver and climbed out of the cab. Glancing up at the classic hotel's brick facade, he dodged yet more tourists and pushed through the double black doors. He crossed the lobby – all dark wood and mood lighting – and got the elevator up to the roof terrace. Checking his watch one last time and pasting a grin on his face, he pushed open the double doors. "SURPRISE!" his family yelled in unison.

Finn grinned and then laughed out loud. "Wow," he said. "I had no idea."

"Oh, of course you did," his grandmother said,

suddenly appearing next to him and kissing him on both cheeks. Finn didn't know how she did it. She always knew. "And what time do you call this? We frightened the life out of the wine waiter half an hour ago."

"Yeah, sorry. The traffic was awful," Finn said.

His gran made a face. "You left late. You were probably..." She took a step back and looked into his eyes and for a moment, Finn was terrified she was going to say 'jerking off', but she didn't, she said, "Studying. You work too hard, you know."

Finn smiled. Wow. Maybe now that he was 18, she couldn't read his mind anymore. But then again, he had actually been studying, kind of. He'd been reading the prospectus for the architecture major at Columbia. It sounded fantastic. His stomach had churned with excitement as he'd read it, but then churned with anxiety when he thought about telling his father he planned to do a Liberal Arts degree. But he wasn't going to think about it tonight.

Finn crossed the room stopping to chat to family members he hadn't seen since he was a child. Uncle Rufus, who moved to Florida after some trouble with the bank he worked for. His new wife, Alice, who didn't actually look much older than Finn, but whose enormous boobs looked brand new. Gran's brother – unfortunately named Johnson – who came to every family party, but only stayed long enough to greet everyone and then no one heard from him again until the next event.

Finn found his parents next to the buffet. They both hugged him.

"You actually looked surprised," his mom smiled. "Well done."

Finn laughed and pulled his surprised face. "I've been working on it."

His dad clapped him on the back. "So what was the hold up?"

Finn blew out a mouthful of air. "Traffic. Plus, you know, I didn't want to get here too early and ruin it. Turned out I left it a bit late."

Finn had just extricated himself from his grandmother's bridge club friends when he spotted Sam crossing the terrace towards him. She was wearing a black, sparkly dress and her hair was piled up messily on her head. She looked incredible. She smiled her heart-racing smile and Finn realised that he'd been staring, open-mouthed. And then he saw Scott just behind her. He was grinning and Finn immediately felt terrible. His best friend. He shouldn't be disappointed to see him, but he kind of was.

"Hey," Finn said as they reached him.

"Hey yourself," Sam said and kissed him on the cheek. "Happy Birthday."

"Thanks." She smelled amazing. He actually, literally felt dizzy. He reached out a hand and grabbed hold of the wall, resisting the urge to touch his face like a moony teenager.

"Hey, man," Scott said. They shook hands and Scott pulled him in for a back-slapping hug before handing him a gift that had clearly been wrapped in-store.

The three of them looked at one another.

"You look gorgeous," Finn said.

"Thanks," Sam said, smiling.

"Er...I was talking to Scott," Finn joked, grinning. "Awkward."

"Ha," Sam said, smiling. "Well I'll leave you two lovebirds alone then. I'm going to go and, you know, powder my proverbial."

"Happy Birthday, man," Scott said, as they both watched Sam leave.

"Thanks."

"You feel different?"

Finn laughed. "Not so much, no. Did you?"

"Course. I felt like A Man."

"And did you get yourself one?" Finn grinned.

"You're funny. If the insurance business doesn't work out, you should think about stand-up."

"I'm thinking about architecture," Finn said and gulped his drink.

"Seriously?"

"Yeah."

"Have you told..?" Scott gestured at pretty much the entire terrace.

"No."

Scott whistled. "Good luck with that."

Finn was stuck on an uncomfortable structural sofa between two of his father's cousins, both of whom were trying to convince him to go into their line of work once he'd graduated from Columbia. His Uncle Mike was something in computers – he'd told Finn what exactly, but Finn hadn't understood much of it. It was sales anyway and Finn knew as confidently as he knew anything that he didn't want to work in sales. His Uncle Dave worked in the nuclear industry. It was the future, he told Finn. Finn wasn't so sure. Just the word "nuclear" suggested the apocalypse to him. He had no interest. He prised himself up with the promise that he'd be back, bearing single malt (it was not only a private party, it was one arranged by his grandmother – he would have no trouble getting served at the bar), but instead he'd wandered over to a more private corner of the terrace and looked out at the view. And there it was. The Empire State Building, the top lit up all white.

He was still staring at it when he heard raised voices. He peered towards the small private lounge that was annexed from the terrace and almost did a double-take. Sam and Scott were standing face-to-face, but Scott had his hands up in front of him, palms towards Sam and she was talking and wiping her face with the heels of her hands. What could have happened? They'd been dancing and kissing last time Finn had seen them. He made himself look away. Both because he felt bad witnessing their row, but also because he felt guilty at the tiny part of him that lit up at the idea that they may break up.

Had Scott really been screwing around? But then why would he tell Sam at Finn's party. Unless he hadn't told her, she'd just found out. Finn looked around – he couldn't see anyone Scott might feasibly be cheating on Sam with. He shook himself. What was he doing? He didn't even know what was going on between them and he was already trying to pair Scott off with someone else.

About ten minutes later, Finn was talking to his mom when Scott interrupted. He looked terrible. He looked like he'd been crying, but he couldn't have been. Scott never cried. At least Finn had never seen him cry in all the years he'd known him.

"I'm sorry, man," he said. "I've got to go. I've—"

"You're leaving?" Finn asked. "Why? What happened?"

"Me and Sam. We had a fight. We – I don't know – she..." He rubbed his face, roughly. "I can't talk about it now. Sorry. I just—"

Finn couldn't pick a coherent thought out of his head, but fortunately his mom stepped in. "That's fine, Scott. If you need to go, you should go. Is everything OK?"

Scott shook his head. "I don't know. But I'm OK. I mean, you don't need to worry."

"OK." She put her hand on Scott's shoulder and gave it a reassuring squeeze, then stepped away, leaving Finn and his best friend alone.

"I feel like a dick leaving your party..." Scott said.

"No, it's fine. You're OK though?" Finn managed

Scott nodded, hugged Finn, and left.

Finn spent the next hour or more talking to various family members. Or rather being talked to by various family members. Everyone wanted to tell him what they thought he should do. Not one mentioned architecture. After a particularly impassioned speech about why he should think about joining the NYPD from a woman he couldn't remember having met in his life before, he extricated himself and headed inside to use the bathroom.

As he walked down the corridor, he was surprised to see Sam coming towards him – he'd assumed she'd left too after her fight with Scott. She had a glass of what looked like champagne in her hand and was smiling weakly at him. Some of her hair had come down and was curling around her shoulders.

"Hey," he said again. Really, he was brilliant.

"Are you enjoying your party?" she asked. She held the champagne glass up.

"I am, thanks. Are you OK?"

Sam leaned against the wall and closed her eyes. "I am." She opened them again. "Your family is lovely."

"Thanks. They're OK, I guess. In small doses."

They both stood there. The beers had obviously dulled his mind. He couldn't think of anything to say.

"So what happened with you and Scott?" Finn asked, eventually.

"Oh," Sam said. "I think it's probably over between us."

"Seriously?" Finn asked. He could feel his legs

shaking. He leaned against the wall too.

Sam nodded. "Yeah. It's just—" she waved the champagne glass again. "You know, one of those things. It's sad, but..." She stared at him.

Finn stared back. Scott and Sam were over. Sam was single. He was staring at her mouth, he realised. He dragged his eyes back up to meet hers and then he leaned forward and kissed her.

She dropped the champagne and the glass shattered on the tile.

"Jesus Christ, Finn!" she said, stepping back.

"I'm sorry," Finn said.

"I thought—" She put her hands up to her face. "I thought we were friends."

"We are," Finn said. "I'm sorry. I just—"

"No," she said. "We're not. Enjoy the rest of your party."

And then she left.

Chapter Fifteen

The play was even better than Jessie remembered it. The actors were more assured and confident. Ben had been good in Manchester, but he was fantastic on Broadway. There'd been some tweaks to the script that made it funnier, sweeter, more thought-provoking. Jessie hadn't given the content of the play much thought over the years, but she had tonight.

It was about how small changes can have a big impact on your life. Small things like buying a different brand of breakfast cereal could turn out to be more important, over the course of a life, than big things like the career you choose. It was about trusting your decisions and letting life unfold.

"That was amazing!" Emma said, as soon as the lights came on. "It was so good!"

"I'm glad you enjoyed it," Natalie said. She looked a bit flushed. Jessie had looked at her a few times during the course of the play and she'd been transfixed, which was amazing really when you thought how many times she'd seen it already.

"What's it like to watch it, knowing you wrote it?" Emma asked.

Jessie had been wondering that too, but she hadn't thought to ask.

Natalie sighed. "Oh it's awful. No matter how many times I see it, I always think of things I'd like to change, or one of the actors gets something wrong, or I just think that tonight is the night everyone will hate it..."

Jessie stared at her mum. She'd never heard her admit anything like that before. "It must be hard..." she started.

"Oh it is," her mum said, wincing. "It's like my baby, you know? It's like you! Like when I took you to nursery for the first time." Natalie smiled. "You were so excited to go and you just ran off, you didn't look back. I stood there and..." She put her hands up to her heart. "I just couldn't believe you were ready to be away from me. It was only then that I realised that *you* might've been ready, but *I* wasn't! I wanted to grab you and run home and make you stay with me!" She laughed, but Jessie couldn't even speak.

"And then," Natalie said, "you ran over towards this wooden slide they had and you tripped on the mat and hit your face and you turned and howled, with your hands up and your eyes closed and I ran over and picked you up."

Jessie bit the inside of her cheek. She wanted to ask what had changed. How her mum had gone from not wanting to leave her at nursery to leaving her and moving across the world? But she didn't want to ask right now.

They stood up and Natalie squeezed Jessie's arm.

"So where's the party?" Emma asked, as they made their way down the stairs.

"Party?" Natalie asked.

"Yes. Ben mentioned the after-party."

Natalie laughed. "Oh, it's not a party. Just some

of the cast and crew usually have a few drinks to help them relax."

"Right," Jessie said. "So where is it?"

"You want to go?"

Jessie and Emma both laughed. "Of course!"

"Oh right. I hadn't thought. You're both underage, of course."

"Mum!" Jessie said.

"OK. But just for half an hour or so; I have to be up early in the morning."

"Do you?" Jessie asked. "What for?"

"To write!" Natalie said, as if it was the most obvious thing in the world.

The "party" was in Ben's dressing room. He was the star of the show and had the biggest dressing room by quite a long way, although it still wasn't big enough for the number of people who'd crammed in, all laughing and talking and drinking. It was thrilling. Jessie felt like she was taking part in a particularly glamorous game of sardines. She lost track of her mum almost immediately, but Emma was squashed up next to her, giving Jessie a running commentary directly into her ear.

"Has that man had Botox, do you think? Or maybe he's just had his ears pinned back?"

"Hmm," Jessie said. "Dunno."

"That's what I've always loved about you. You're such a sparkling conversationalist. Oh dear." Emma nodded at another woman who was showing a lot of cleavage and belly. "Do you think she meant to put that top on the other way around?"

Jessie was watching Ben. He was leaning up against the window ledge and drinking from a bottle of beer. He kept glancing over and smiling. She needed to get over there and talk to him, but how was she going to do that? Crowd-surf?

"He keeps looking at you," Emma whispered.

"He does, doesn't he?" Jessie whispered back.

"Go and talk to him."

"Yeah, I know. But how?"

"Oh! I know! Give him a come hither look and then go out to the loo and he'll follow you."

"A 'come hither' look? Yeah, OK, Jane Austen. But what if he doesn't follow?"

"Well then when you come back you just

squeeze right over there instead of joining me here in bitchy corner."

"Right," Jessie said. "I'm doing it. Wish me luck."

"You don't say that in the theatre, darling," Emma said, dramatically. "Break a leg! But not literally."

Jessie shuffled out of the dressing room and made her way along the corridor to the bathrooms. Once she'd been to the loo, she stood in front of the mirror and appraised her appearance. She looked good. She'd caught the sun and looked healthier than she did in Manchester. She still wished she'd brought some make-up with her though, or at least thought to borrow Emma's lip-gloss. She pulled her hair down from its ponytail and fluffed it up with her hands, then she bit her lips, pinched her cheeks and smoothed her eyebrows. After rearranging her boobs in her bra and sniffing under her arms, she headed back to the party.

As she passed the small make-up room next to Ben's dressing room, something caught Jessie's eye. She stopped and looked through the half-open door. Reflected in the mirror above the make-up table, she could see a couple having a full-on snog.

She smiled. They'd obviously moved away from the party for privacy. Maybe she and Ben could do the same. He'd know where to take her where no one would see them. She felt the butterflies flicker again. Could he really be interested in her? Was she really going to go for it?

She heard Natalie's voice and looked around. She sounded close, but Jessie couldn't see her. And then she felt her stomach clench. She pushed open the door to the make-up room and looked at what she'd already seen reflected in the mirror. Even so, it took a couple of seconds for her brain to catch up, but once it had she stumbled back into the corridor, her eyes filling with tears.

Had they seen her? She waited, but they obviously hadn't. She had to get out. She had to get Emma.

She made it halfway into Ben's dressing room and managed to pull Emma towards her. "We have to go," she called.

"What?!" Emma said.

"I'll tell you in a minute. We just have to go. Please, Em."

"OK. Where's your mum?"

"Not Mum. Just us. Come on."

Once they were in the corridor, Jessie shushed Emma and pulled her towards the exit. Out on the street, Jessie felt the tears she'd been holding back start to flow.

"Jess! What happened?" Emma put her arm around her.

"We need to go," Jessie sobbed.

"I'll get a cab."

Jessie leaned back against the theatre and closed her eyes. She couldn't believe what had happened. She couldn't believe she'd thought Ben was interested in her. How could she be so stupid? Why was she always so stupid?

"I think we should walk up to Broadway," Emma said. "OK?"

Jessie nodded. Emma linked her arm through Jessie's and they started walking the short distance to the main road.

"She's with Ben," Jessie said, before sobbing again.

"Who?"

"Mum. She's with Ben."

Emma stopped walking and looked at her friend. "Your mum?! With Ben? Where?"

Jessie sighed, raggedly. "They were in the next room. She was sitting on his knee. Kissing."

"What?!" Emma said.

"What is wrong with her?" Jessie said. "Why can't she just be a normal mum? Why can't she be like *your* mum?"

They spotted a cab with its light on. Emma waved it over and they clambered in.

"72nd and Broadway," Emma said.

"No!" Jessie almost shouted. "I'm not going back there."

"So where are we going to go?" Emma asked.

"Yeah," the driver said. "Where ya gonna go?"

"What's a really nice hotel?" Jessie asked him. "Expensive."

He shrugged. "The Campbell's real nice."

Chapter Sixteen

After Sam left, Finn went down to the lobby, partly hoping that she might still be there and that he could apologise properly, but mainly just avoiding his party, his family and friends.

What had he been thinking of? To just kiss her. Just like that. Even if she had been interested in him – and it didn't seem like she ever had been – that would not have been the time. But she'd been standing there, looking so gorgeous, with her big blue eyes and he'd just thought...well, he hadn't thought. He'd just kissed her.

And he hadn't even thought about Scott. His best friend. His best friend who was clearly devastated by whatever had happened with Sam, but Finn hadn't even given him a second's thought. What kind of a friend was he?

He dropped his head into his hands. What a mess. What if she told Scott? Yeah, she'd said it was over, but that didn't mean it was. That just meant they'd had a row. She was probably heading over to Scott's right that minute to tell him what an asshole his supposed best friend was. And he felt like an asshole. He did. Happy 18th birthday.

"What on earth are you doing down here?"

Finn looked up to see his grandmother striding across the lobby towards him.

"I just—" he started.

"Just nothing, Finn. Please go back to your party. You've been missed."

Finn rubbed the back of his neck and then stood up. "Sorry."

His grandmother sighed. "OK. Sit down. What's wrong? Are you having some sort of...existential crisis?"

Finn laughed. "No. Not really."

"Then what is it? You haven't enjoyed the party—"

Finn started to protest, but she interrupted him. "Now, now. I can tell. I've known you since you were a zygote, remember? I know when you're enjoying yourself and tonight you've been wearing the same expression you used to wear whenever I took you to the Plaza for brunch."

Finn smiled. He'd always hated those overly formal Plaza brunches. Waiters hovering around the tables to put the napkins on your lap and a replica of the hotel sculpted out of butter. But the worst thing about them was that was always when his gran used to give him the benefit of her life experience, which was almost always along the lines of 'you must do what is expected of you, whether or not it makes you happy.' If he told his gran he was considering changing his major, she'd have a fit.

"Is it a girl?" his grandmother asked.

"What?" Finn asked, his mind back with the architecture prospectus.

"The reason you can't seem to enjoy this wonderful party I'm throwing for you: is it a girl?"

"Sort of," Finn said.

"Oh Finn! There will be plenty of time for moping

around after girls. You've got everything in front of you! You're 18! You're going to Columbia!"

Finn smiled. "I know. I just...I made a fool of myself, that's all."

"Oh well, everyone does that. You have to make a fool of yourself once or twice. It's part of the fun. Is she here, this girl?"

Finn shook his head.

"Well then. Put her out of your mind. Come back up to the terrace. Have a drink, eat some cake. Did I tell you that Arthur is here? Professor McLoughlin? I'll introduce you."

She linked arms with her grandson and led him towards the elevator.

Chapter Seventeen

Jessie and Emma sat in silence all the way downtown. Emma squeezed her friend's hand while Jessie stared out of the cab window, her tears blurring the city lights, making them dance in front of her eyes. This wasn't what was supposed to happen. This summer was supposed to be about her, not her mother. Why was it always about her mother?

They pulled up in front of the hotel and Jessie was practically through the double doors before Emma had even got out of the cab. Emma caught up with her in the foyer.

"We can't stay in a hotel," Emma said.

"We can," Jess said. "I've got the emergency credit card."

"But your mum'll think something's happened to us."

"Tough," Jessie said. "She should've thought of that before then, shouldn't she?"

"Come on, Jess," she said, grabbing her friend's arm. "Let's just go home and talk to her. And your dad's coming tomorrow. You'll feel better when you've seen your dad."

"I don't want to talk to her. She doesn't care about me. She never has."

"You know that's not true."

"She's sleeping with Ben! He's my age! I thought—" Jessie started to cry again.

"I know," Emma said, guiding Jessie over to one of the leather sofas, artfully placed at intervals around the large space.

"I thought he liked me," Jessie said, sniffing.

"I thought so too," Emma said. They sat down and Emma put her arm around Jessie.

"Why doesn't she care about me?" Jessie asked in a small voice.

"She does. Of course she does. You heard her before, talking about your first day at nursery."

"Yes, cos it reminded her of the play. She cares more about the play than she does about me."

"I don't think she does. I'm sure that if it came down to it – if she had to choose – she'd choose you."

"She didn't though, did she? She chose the play. She chose New York. I thought she'd chosen Jack, but she obviously chose *Ben* too."

"That's not true though, is it?" Emma said, quietly. "You chose to stay with your dad. You could've come to New York, couldn't you?"

"It was GCSEs! How could I have left then? I didn't have a choice. What would you have done?"

"I don't know," Emma said. "But I think you need to go and talk to her now. We can't stay here."

"We can! We've got the credit card—"

"Which is for emergencies—"

"And why not let her worry about me for a change? That's if she even notices I've gone..."

"Jess. Come on. We're not staying here. Let's just get a cab back up to your mum's. You don't even need to talk to her tonight. Talk to her tomorrow.

But I don't want to stay here. Really."

Jessie put her head in her hands. She really didn't want to go back. She didn't want to face her mum. And what if Ben was there? How could she have been so stupid? Again. First Taylor and now this. Did she just have terrible taste or was she sending out some sort of idiot signal.

"I don't want to go back yet. Don't make me go back yet."

Emma frowned. "OK. We'll stay here for a bit. But you need to ring your mum." She looked around the foyer and then stood up. "I'm going for a wee."

"OK." Jess got her phone out of her pocket and noticed her hands were shaking. She scrolled down and chose her mum's number. She answered on the second ring.

"Mum?" Jessie's voice cracked.

"Where the HELL are you?!" Natalie shouted.

Jessie held the phone away from her ear. "It's OK, we're fine. We're—"

"It's NOT OK! It's not OK, Jess! I've been worried sick! Can you hear me? You walked out of the theatre without a word. I didn't know what happened to you.

I didn't know where the hell you'd gone. I didn't even know that you *had* gone!"

"No," Jessie said, her eyes filling. "You wouldn't."

"And where are you now?" Natalie went on as if she hadn't even heard Jessie speak. "This is New York, this isn't Manchester. You can't walk around in the middle of the bloody night!"

"You can't do that in Manchester either," Jessie said.

"Don't get smart with me. Don't you DARE get smart with me. I am your mother!"

"Yeah," Jessie said. "When it suits you."

She pressed end on the call and dropped her head into her hands. She was still sitting like that when Emma got back.

"She's fine," Jessie lied. "She was worried, but I told her where we are and that we'll get a taxi back and she's fine."

"Really?" Emma said.

"Yeah. I mean, she was annoyed that I didn't tell her we were going, but she's OK as long as we get a cab and we're not too late. I think maybe Ben's there..." Jessie felt guilty about lying to her best friend, but she just couldn't face her mum right then.

"Oh, right. So...what do you want to do?" Emma asked.

Jessie looked around the foyer and then noticed the hotel directory on the wall.

"Look." She pointed at it.

"What?"

"Roof terrace."

"It'll be closed now, surely."

"Well, we could go up and have a look. Imagine the view."

Emma rolled her eyes. "You and views. OK. Let's go. But we're not going near the edge."

Chapter Eighteen

Finn was listening to his friend Eric talking about a gig he'd been to where someone had puked on his shoes. Or maybe he'd puked on someone else's shoes. Finn wasn't *really* listening, so he wasn't sure. He was thinking about Sam. And about changing his major. And about kissing Sam. And telling his parents that he'd changed his major. And telling Scott that he'd kissed Sam. The two subjects swirled around in his head until he wanted to put his hands over his ears and shout 'SHUT UP!' Maybe he would. It was his party, he could freak out if he wanted to, couldn't he?

No. He couldn't. His parents were there. His

grandmother. Professor whatever-his-name-was. He had to be mature and responsible. Should an 18th party be like that? Shouldn't he be off raising hell somewhere? Weren't there some shoes he should be puking on?

Frowning, he ran his hands through his hair.

Eric wandered off to get another drink and Finn's gran brought the Professor – Professor McLoughlin – over to talk to him. Although Finn's input wasn't really required. His gran talked Finn up and the Professor talked Columbia up, while Finn nodded and smiled and tried to get the cacophony in his head to shut up.

Eventually they left too and Finn was, at last, alone. He looked around at his friends and family. He loved them all. He did. He wished he could appreciate that more when he was actually with them. And then he saw two girls he didn't know. Or at least, he wasn't sure who they were. One of them looked familiar though. They stopped and looked around. Then the one with the long, blonde hair – the one he thought he'd seen before – looked straight at him. And smiled.

***

In the lift, Jessie worried about what her mum would do when they got back to the apartment. She'd never been all that good at discipline – preferring to leave it to Jessie's dad while she got on with writing – but Jessie knew she had a temper and she'd sounded furious on the phone.

And Jessie also knew that Emma wouldn't be impressed when she realised she'd lied to her. Emma wouldn't want to upset Natalie when she was in New York as her guest for the summer. Jessie had put her best friend in a difficult position, she knew. And what if Natalie sent them both home? But she wouldn't go that far. Surely.

And then there was Ben. How could she have thought he was interested in her? He'd never really given any indication, had he? Why couldn't she have proper relationships with nice boys who actually liked her instead of imaginary relationships with boys who were either only interested in one thing or not interested at all? But why had he taken them to the zoo? That was the one thing she couldn't understand. Unless. Unless he'd been on his way there to see Natalie. Jessie mentally slapped herself. *Of course* that was the explanation. He hadn't even wanted to spend time with her after all, it was just a decoy when he'd arrived at the apartment and bumped into them. How humiliating.

She was so tired of thinking and worrying about it all. She wished there was a switch she could press to get the noise in her head to stop. Or even a volume button so she could dial it right down and let some other, nicer, thoughts in.

The lift pinged and Jessie and Emma stepped out onto the roof terrace. Emma pointed at a board stating they'd arrived at Finn's 18th birthday party, but Jessie just shrugged. No one was blocking their way. No one was telling them they had to leave. And there was probably a free bar.

She looked around. It was pretty busy.

And then she saw him. He was standing on his own and looking straight at her. She smiled.

He smiled back.

Chapter Nineteen

They each took a few steps until they were standing close enough to speak.

"I think I know you from somewhere," Jessie said.

He smiled. "I was just thinking that about you."

They smiled at each other.

"So I've had a really crappy night," Finn said. "How about you?"

Jessie and Emma both laughed.

"The boy I thought liked me is actually with my mother," Jessie said.

"I kissed my best friend's girlfriend and she dropped her drink and ran out of the building," Finn replied.

"Bloody hell," Emma said. "And I was feeling hard done by cos I left my lipgloss in the taxi."

The three of them laughed.

"Do you want to come and sit down?" Finn asked. "I'm Finn, by the way. This is my party."

The girls introduced themselves and followed Finn round to the more private area of the terrace. Once Jessie had swooned at the view of the Empire State Building, they sat down.

"So what happened to you?" Jessie asked. "Who's the girl?"

"Sam," Finn said. "My friend Scott's girlfriend. I've liked her for a long time. It just crept up on me, you know? Obviously I knew she was gorgeous and she's really cool, but I then I started hoping I'd bump into her when Scott wasn't around." He blew out a long breath. "And then tonight she said it was over between her and Scott. And I don't know what happened. I was looking at her and she was looking at me and then I kissed her. And she freaked."

"Wow," Jessie said.

"Yeah," Finn shrugged. "She dropped her glass and stormed out."

"Do you think she'll tell her boyfriend?" Emma asked.

"I don't know," he said. "Would you?"

Emma and Jessie looked at each other.

"I don't know," Jessie said. "I guess it depends how much she actually likes you. You might've just shocked her and once she calms down she'll realise she overreacted and it'll all be fine."

"Or," Emma said, pulling an apologetic face. "Or she'll tell him straight away as a way of getting back with him or back at him. How good a friend is Scott?"

"The best. I'm such a dick."

"You can't choose who you fall for," Jessie said.

"Really?" Emma asked, raising one eyebrow.

"What?" Jessie said.

"Well not long ago you were insisting your mum was kissing Ben to spite you."

"Oh, shut up," Jessie said, not meanly. "I didn't say it was to spite me anyway, just that she never gives me a thought."

"My dad's a bit like that," Finn said. "Not that he doesn't think about me, but that he doesn't think about the real me. You know? He's got a Finn in his head and that Finn is nothing like me."

"What's the Finn in his head like?" Jessie asked.

Finn smiled. "A younger version of himself, I think."

"And he wants you to do the things he didn't do himself?" Emma asked.

"Not really, no. He wants me to do exactly what he did."

"And what's that?"

"Insurance."

Emma and Jessie both winced.

"Wow. Live the dream," Jessie said and they laughed.

"I know, right?"

"What about your mom?" Finn asked. "She wants you to be like her?"

"I don't think so," Jessie said. "It's more that she thinks everything revolves around her. When people do things they're doing them to her. Even when it's nothing to do with her. She needs to realise I have my own life and I can make my own decisions and it's not always about her. You know

Finn nodded. "So who's the boy? You said the boy you liked is with your mom?"

"He's the lead in the play she wrote."

"Your mom wrote a play?" Finn said.

"Yeah. It's on Broadway. That's why me and Emma are here for the summer. 'Cos she lives here now."

"What play?" Finn asked.

"*Small Change*?"

"*Small Change*? I love that play! My mom's a theatre critic. She loved it and made me go see it. I can't believe your mom wrote it!"

"Yeah," Jessie said, dryly. "She's great."

Finn laughed. "A great writer but not such a great mom?"

Jessie laughed too. "Yeah. Not such a great mom."

"And the lead? Isn't he pretty young."

"Yep. My age, more or less."

"And when you say he's 'with' her?"

Jessie sighed. "I saw them together. I was on my way to, you know, see if he was interested. In me. And instead I found her sitting on his knee, his shirt untucked, her hands all over him."

"Jeez," Finn said.

Jessie nodded. "It's just...I mean, thank God I hadn't got the chance to say anything to him! Can you imagine how humiliating that would be? 'Er. Might you be interested in me at all?' 'Oh sorry. Maybe if I wasn't shagging your mum.'" She shuddered.

Finn rolled his shoulders back and cracked his neck one way and then the other. "This is probably going to sound weird, but is your dad an architect?" he asked Jessie.

Jessie's eyebrows shot up in surprise. "He is, yeah. How do you know that?"

"I overheard the two of you talking in the street. I thought you looked familiar when you first came in, but I only just realised for sure. You were looking up at the Empire State Building."

Jessie stared at him. "I don't think that's where I know you from." She kept staring, taking advantage of the opportunity to study Finn's face. He was really good-looking – deep brown eyes and great cheekbones. Cheekbones!

"The deli!" Jessie almost shouted. "You were sitting in the window. We took your table. You said hi."

"Gino's?" Finn asked, grinning. "Yeah! That's up near our apartment. The Albright."

"No way," Jessie said. "That's where my mum lives too."

They grinned at each other until Emma coughed. "Hadn't we better be getting back?" she asked.

Jessie put the key in the door, half-expecting Natalie to yank it open from the other side, but the apartment was quiet. She wasn't in the living room and she wasn't in the kitchen. Surely she wasn't working.

"She must've gone to bed," Emma said.

Jessie nodded, but she didn't think she really had.

Emma went to the bathroom and Jessie knocked on her mum's office door. There was no reply, but Jessie pushed it open anyway.

"I don't want to discuss it now," Natalie said, without turning round.

"Mum—"

She turned and Jessie was shocked to see her mum had been crying.

"Not tonight, Jessie! We'll talk about it in the

morning. Go to bed."

Jessie took a step backwards and pulled the door closed. She felt sick. She felt guilty. She went into the lounge and opened the window with the Juliet balcony. She leaned out as far as she dared and looked down at Broadway.

Her mum had been crying. Her mum hardly ever cried. But she'd also been kissing Ben! Was Jessie supposed to just forget about that? Was she supposed to just say, "Oh right. Your boyfriend's my age? How very Demi Moore of you. Lots of luck to you both!" She knew it wasn't her mum's fault Jessie had thought she had a chance with Ben. And it wasn't her mum's fault that she'd humiliated herself with Taylor either. But it was her mum's fault that she wasn't around. It was her mum's fault that she was thousands of miles away. Weren't mothers supposed to teach daughters about boys? About relationships? And sex?

"Are you OK?" she heard Emma ask.

She closed the windows. "Yeah. Mum's in her office. She doesn't want to talk to me."

"I thought you said she was fine with it," Emma

said. She'd washed off her make-up and she looked really young.

"I lied," Jessie said. "I'm sorry. I just didn't want to come back. Can we...can we not talk about it now?"

Emma sighed. "I can't believe you lied to me."

"I know," Jessie said. "I'm sorry. I really am. I just...I just want this day to be over. Can we talk tomorrow."

Emma sat down next to Jessie and hugged her. "No problem."

Chapter Twenty

Finn woke up with that horrible sensation that something terrible had happened, but he wasn't sure what. And then it came flooding back. He kissed Sam. He cringed with the embarrassment. He kissed Sam and now he had to deal with Scott. He had no idea what he was going to say to him. Should he tell him? Or wait to see if Sam told him. Maybe if they really were broken up, she wouldn't say anything. But could he take that chance? He'd usually go downtown to meet the two of them for brunch, but he guessed that wouldn't be happening. Maybe he could just stay in bed...

***

Jessie woke up with that horrible sensation that something terrible had happened, but she wasn't sure what. And then it came flooding back. The play and then thinking something could happen with Ben (idiot!). Finding her mum kissing Ben and – even worse – with her hand down his trousers. Jessie shuddered. And then her mum's face when she'd got back to the apartment. Tearful. Disappointed. Jessie cringed. She was going to have to face her and the thought made her not want to get out of bed.

In the shower, Finn's mind ran over the events of the previous night again and again. Scott's face. Sam's face. Sam dropping the glass. His grandmother telling him to, basically, do his duty. No change there. But then Jessie. At the thought of Jessie, he felt the corners of his mouth quirk up. She was nice. She'd made him feel better about everything. And she was somewhere in this apartment building. He wondered what she was doing.

Jessie forced herself to get out of bed and into the shower. Emma was still asleep and she didn't know whether her mum was up or not, but she knew she would have to face her eventually and she needed a shower to wake up. Under the hot water, her mind ran over the events of the previous night again and again. Her mum sitting on Ben's lap. Running out of the theatre. The taxi ride to the hotel. And then Finn. At the thought of Finn, she felt the corners of her mouth quirk up. He was nice. He'd made her feel better about everything. And he was somewhere in this apartment building. She wondered what he was doing.

Chapter Twenty-One

Natalie was sitting at the kitchen table. She looked tired and drained. Jessie felt another pang of guilt.

"Look, mum," she said.

Natalie held up one hand and sighed. "Jessie. I don't really feel in the mood to talk to you right now. I'm tired. I'm disappointed. And I haven't even had a cup of coffee."

"But you keep saying that. You keep saying 'not now'. Are we going to talk about it? Are you going to...punish me or something? Because if you are, I think you need to get on with it."

"Why?" Natalie said. "Why do I need to get on with

it? Because it's inconvenient for you not knowing what I'm planning to do? Well, guess what? That's just tough."

"Fine!" Jessie said. She stormed into the bedroom, slamming the door behind her.

"God!" she heard from Emma's bed. Emma's face appeared from out of the covers. "I was asleep! You scared the crap out of me!"

"Sorry," Jessie said angrily before throwing herself face down on her bed.

"What's happened?" Emma croaked.

"Nothing. She won't talk to me. Not until she's had her coffee. She's being all..." Jessie groped for the word. "Passive-aggressive."

Emma snorted.

"What?" Jessie asked, rolling over onto her back.

"That's obviously where you get it from."

"What?"

"How passive-aggressive was storming off to stay in a hotel instead of talking to your mum last night?"

"It's hardly the same," Jessie said.

Emma laughed. "It is the same. You ran away

instead of dealing with her and she hid in her office instead of dealing with you."

Emma pulled the covers back over her head.

Jessie lay, staring up at the ceiling. Maybe Emma was right. Had she ever told her mum how she felt? How hurt she'd been when she moved to New York and left her in Manchester? No, she hadn't. She'd acted like it was all fine with her, that it didn't bother her at all, and then behaved like a brat. But it went back even further than that, didn't it? She'd never told her mum how she'd felt growing up. How she never felt like her mum had any time for her. She'd taken advantage of it by getting her mum to agree to things she wouldn't have otherwise agreed to, but at the same time she'd resented her for it. And, no, she'd never told her.

Jessie rolled over onto her side and pulled her knees up to her chest. She should tell her. It was like Finn had said last night about his dad. Something about how his dad never thought about the 'real Finn'. That he had a Finn in his head that was nothing like the Finn in reality.

The mum in Jessie's head was self-centred and didn't care about Jessie at all. But she knew that wasn't really true. Not really. She had the photo in her office. And there was that thing she'd said about crying in the loos at Jessie's leavers' assembly. Jessie had resented her for that for years, but she'd been wrong. What else might she have been wrong about?

She shuffled up the bed and leaned back against the pillows. She wasn't wrong about what had happened last night. She just wasn't. Her mum had been kissing and feeling up a twenty-year-old boy. She really had. But it wasn't her mum's fault that Jessie had thought she was in with a chance with Ben. Her mum didn't even know that. Jessie was acting like her mum had stolen Ben from her when that wasn't the case at all.

"Em," Jessie said.

"Whaa?"

"What do you think about Mum and Ben?"

There was a groan from under the covers and then Emma's face appeared. "I think it was a shock to you. You fancied Ben and you thought maybe he liked you too. Of course it was going to be a shock that he actually likes your mum. And then there's the fact that he's our age, pretty much. That's a bit of a surprise too. Finding out your mum's a cougar."

"Oh my God!" Jessie cried. "Don't call her that!"

"And of course it'll always be a shock when you see your mum feeling someone up. Whether it's your dad or..." Emma shuffled up the bed. "Oh great. Now I'm thinking about my mum and dad at it. Pass me something to puke in."

Jessie smiled. "But what I'm thinking is, it's not about me. Yes, it was a shock and everything, but she didn't do it to hurt me. Any of it."

Emma smiled at her friend. "Exactly."

Chapter Twenty-Two

When Finn got out of the shower, he found a message on his phone from Scott. He rang him back and they arranged to meet in midtown, pretty much halfway between their apartments.

Finn got the subway, which he regretted almost instantly. It was ridiculously hot and airless, like travelling in a sauna. Everyone looked listless, fanning themselves with sections from the paper, or just leaning back against the window, their eyes closed. By the time he arrived at the Rockefeller Center stop, it was all he could do to drag himself up the steps and onto the street.

When he arrived at the Ferrante, a diner they'd been going to on and off for years, Scott was already there. He had a cup of coffee and a hangdog expression on his face.

"Hey," he said, glancing up.

Finn dropped into the seat opposite. He almost felt like this was a mafia-style "sit down". But Scott was his oldest friend. Even if Sam *had* told him about the kiss, he'd give Finn a chance to explain, wouldn't he?

"So. Are you OK?" Finn asked.

Scott looked up again, just as a waitress appeared next to them. They both ordered and then Scott said, "She's moving back to LA."

For a second, Finn thought he meant the waitress and wondered how Scott knew and if she was an actress, but then he realised. Sam.

"What? When?"

"She decided when she was just back there. She's transferring to UCLA."

"Wow. When did she tell you?"

"At your party."

"Jeez. No wonder you left. Why did she tell you there?"

"She didn't mean to. She let it slip. I can't remember exactly what she said. But I asked her what she meant – I thought she'd arranged to maybe do a semester there or something – and she told me."

"I'm really sorry, man."

"Yeah."

The waitress arrived with a coffee for Finn. He added sugar and thought about Sam. She was leaving. It was probably best. For him. Not for Scott. So did that mean he didn't need to tell Scott anything? It didn't seem like Sam had anyway. He felt relieved. And then he felt guilty for feeling relieved.

"You haven't thought about doing the long-distance thing? I mean, you go out to your dad a lot anyway."

Scott rubbed his face. "Nah. She doesn't want to. I mean, I don't either. I think we're too young for that. And I was so pissed at her last night, man. I think it's over anyway."

"She knew you'd be pissed though, right?"

Scott laughed. "No. She thought I'd be happy for her." He raised one eyebrow. "I mean, I do feel bad. She's excited and I just crapped all over it. But what did she expect?"

Finn took a gulp of his coffee. He'd added too much sugar. "I'm sorry, man," he said again. "That sucks."

"Yeah. I really liked her, you know?"

"Yeah," Finn said. "Me too."

They sat in silence for a few minutes, while Finn drank his oversweetened coffee and then Scott said, "I'm not going to college in September."

"What?" Finn said.

"I'm going to keep working, for at least another year."

"What? Why?"

"They've made me assistant manager. The money's pretty good. I'll be able to save for when I do actually go next year."

"But your parents have a college fund, don't they?" Finn asked.

"Yeah, but it's not enough. It was invested and, I don't know, there's some issue. And I like working. It's just another year."

"So that's why you've been working so much?"

Scott nodded.

"Why didn't you just tell me?"

Scott shook his head. "I was embarrassed. You were trying to work out what you want to do – thinking about changing your major, dealing with your parents – I just...I didn't want to say anything until it was definite."

Finn stared at his friend. He couldn't believe he'd spent the last few months risking their friendship over Sam.

"Congratulations on the promotion, I guess," he said.

Scott laughed. "Thanks, man."

Jessie knocked on her mum's office door and then, when there was no reply, rested her forehead against it. She didn't want to just go in. Not if her mum didn't want her there. But she really wanted to talk to her. She knocked again.

"I'm here," Natalie said.

Jessie turned round. Her mum was standing in the doorway of her bedroom. Her eyes were red-rimmed again and her hair was all stuck up at one side.

"I wanted to talk to you," Jessie said.

"Me too," her mum said. She ran her hands

through her hair. "I was going to wait until your dad got here, but I think maybe we should talk first."

Jessie nodded.

"Shall I make us some coffee or something?" Natalie asked.

Jessie nodded again and sat down at the kitchen table. She felt nervous. In fact, she felt like she was going to be sick. Was this normal? To feel so terrified of having a conversation with your own mother? Maybe it was. Particularly when she knew how much she had to say.

Natalie made the coffee in silence and then sat down opposite Jessie. "So," she said. "I'll start. You frightened me half to death last night. I had no idea where you were. I was worried sick."

Jessie stared down at a place mat with a print of the Manhattan skyline around the edge.

"I'm sorry," she said.

"You—" Natalie started and then must have realised that Jessie had apologised. She reached over and touched the back of Jess's hand with her index finger. "Just tell me what happened."

Jess closed her eyes and then took a deep breath. "I saw you. With Ben."

"Oh," Natalie said. "I didn't realise. I'm so sorry. I—"

"No," Jessie interrupted. "I overreacted."

She looked at her mum: two pink smudges had appeared on Natalie's cheeks.

"And I thought he might like me," Jessie said.

"Oh, Jess," Natalie said. "I'm so sorry. I had no idea. What did you... I mean, where were we, when you saw us?"

"It was in the room next to his dressing room," Jessie said. She glanced up at her mum and back down again.

"Oh God," Natalie said.

"How long have you two been, you know?"

Natalie blew out a breath. "Since not long after we came out here."

"Bloody hell!" Jessie said.

"I know. I should have told you. I just... He's 20. And you and I haven't exactly talked. Not about anything important, I mean."

"Wow. I thought you were with Jack," Jessie

said. "I thought you'd been with him since you first put on the play."

"My God, really? God, no. Jack's gay!"

"He is not!" Jessie said. "Is he?"

Her mum nodded. "Absolutely."

"Well I wish I'd known that two years ago," Jessie said. "Although I probably would have thought he was going out with Dad..."

Natalie smiled. "I phoned your dad last night."

Jessie winced. "What did he say?"

"He said not to worry. That you were very mature and sensible and I should trust you."

"Did he?" Jessie said. "Bloody hell."

"I didn't react very well, I'm afraid. I was upset and worried about you and it just felt like your dad was..." She sighed. "Like he was telling me I don't know my own daughter. But I don't. Do I?"

Jessie fiddled with the handle of her coffee cup. She noticed her hand was shaking. "Probably not, no."

"I know you resent me," Natalie said. "That's why I really wanted you to come for the summer. I wanted to try and...not make it up to you, but to show you that we could still be friends."

"But I don't want us to be friends!" Jessie said. "I've got friends. I need a mum."

"I know. I'm just not very good at that. I never really was."

They sat in silence for a couple of minutes. Natalie drank her coffee. Jessie sloshed hers around in the cup.

"Why didn't you want me to come to New York with you in the first place?" Jessie said, eventually.

Natalie shook her head. "I did. Jess, I promise you, I did."

"I didn't feel like you did," Jessie said. "It was like the very last thing you said."

Natalie chewed her lip. "OK. I *did* want you to. I knew how obsessed you were with this place. But also I wanted you to be secure. I thought you'd be happier in Manchester with your dad. I know that it wasn't my call to make, I should have talked to you about it, but like I just said, I'm not very good at this. I work all the time. It's hard to be a a full-time parent too."

"Dad works too," Jessie said. "And I don't need a full-time parent. Just a part-time one would be fine."

"When your dad stops working, he stops working," Natalie said. "I just can't switch myself off like that. I'm sorry, but I can't. I am trying though."

"I used to think you didn't care about me at all," Jessie said, finally.

Natalie's eyes filled with tears. "You did? Oh Jess. I'm so sorry."

"You were always working."

"I know. I wanted everything to be better for you. I wanted us to have money, for one. And I thought it was important that you see that I was happy with what I was doing, but—"

"You just did it *all* the time!"

"I know. I'm sorry. I really regret that. All that time I was writing *Small Change*... I was obsessed with it. I really was. But I wasn't there for you. Which is so insane because if it wasn't for you I never would have written it."

"What? Why?" Jessie asked.

"You probably don't remember...or maybe you do. I don't think we've ever talked about it. But we were coming back to the cottage – in Caernarfon, you remember? It was just me and you. Your dad had stayed behind, engrossed in some book or something – and I parked the car and said "Hop out" to you. And you did. You just hopped straight out and this car – this man from the next cottage along – just flew past and came so close to hitting you. Literally if you'd taken one step away from the car he would have smashed straight into you and he was going too fast, we'd already commented on it, your dad and I, about how fast he was driving and how we should probably have said something. But you shrieked and then laughed and I shrieked and hugged you and it was all fine, but then that night I started thinking about what could have happened."

She reached over and took Jessie's hand. "If we'd got back seconds earlier and you'd taken that step he would have hit you. And I couldn't stop going over it. If we'd parked in a different spot or if I hadn't looked at myself in the mirror in the visor or if there hadn't been someone in front of us in the queue or if I'd had the right change when I paid and I kept thinking of all these different factors. All these tiny things, any of which could have made the difference between you being alive and being dead.

I couldn't stop thinking about it to the point where I couldn't sleep. So I got up in the night and started writing – and I found that I couldn't stop. That's what eventually became *Small Change*."

"Wow," Jessie said. Her eyes had filled with tears. "So I should probably get a percentage, right?"

The door buzzed and made them both jump.

"Saved by the buzzer," Natalie said, smiling. "That'll be your dad."

Chapter Twenty-Three

"Hey, sweetie," Jessie's dad said, as he walked into the apartment.

He opened his arms and Jessie rushed straight round the table and let him hug her. She felt him kiss the top of her head and she held on tight. She didn't want to let go. She hadn't realised how much she'd missed him. Her dad gave her one more squeeze and then gently pushed her away.

"You really frightened your mum," he said.

"I know," Jessie said.

"It's OK," Natalie said. "We've been talking and I think..." She looked at Jessie. "I think we're OK, aren't we?"

Jessie nodded. "There's something I want to talk to the two of you about though," she said.

"That sounds ominous," her dad said. "Can I get a cup of coffee first?"

"Of course," Jessie said. She sat down and while her mum made her dad a coffee, Jessie asked about the journey and after Rhys, who'd gone straight to their hotel. And then her mum sat down and both of her parents looked at Jessie expectantly.

"This is hard," she said. "I don't really know where to start."

"Just tell us," her dad said.

"I've been thinking that I'd like to...stay here. Move here. To New York."

Her parents looked at each other and then back at her.

"Dad, I love you and I love living with you, but I don't know what I'm going to do in Manchester. Since I've been here, I've felt...different. I feel like New York's where I'm meant to be. I've looked into it a bit and I could finish school here. But obviously I'd have to live with Mum."

"I would love that," Natalie said. "I really would."

John rubbed his face with both hands and then smiled. "Well, I wasn't going to say anything until everything was finalised, but I'm not just here to visit you, my gorgeous daughter. I'm actually having meetings about setting up a New York branch of the office."

"No way," Jessie said.

"I've been worrying about how I would tell you that we may have to move to New York, but..."

Jessie jumped up and ran around the table to hug her dad. "Oh my God!"

"So you're happy then?" he asked, smiling.

"That's wonderful," Natalie said. "But does that mean you won't want to live with me?"

"Oh," Jessie said. She walked back round to her seat and sat. "I don't know."

"Well we don't have to decide now, do we?" John said. "Like I say, it's not final yet, but who knows, maybe me and Rhys could get a place in this building..."

Natalie snorted. "I think that might be a bit too close..."

"Does Dad know about..." Jessie suddenly thought to ask her mum.

Natalie's eyebrows shot up.

"About what?" John asked.

"Ben and I are...a couple," Natalie said, studying her coffee cup.

John laughed. "What? Isn't he, like, 18?"

Natalie looked up. "He's 20. And isn't Rhys, like, a man?"

Jessie laughed and her parents both looked at her.

"You have to admit, Dad," she said. "That was a good one."

"Jesus," John said. "Is it serious?"

Natalie nodded. "It is, yes."

"Wow. OK then. Well, I guess as long as you're happy..."

"I am," Natalie said. "Actually, I think we should all go out for dinner together. Tomorrow night, perhaps – give everyone a chance to get used to the idea."

"*All* of us?" Jessie asked.

Natalie nodded. "Me and Ben. Your dad and Rhys. You and Emma."

"If she ever wakes up," Jessie said.

"I think it will be good for us to all sit down together and talk," Natalie said.

"Or it could be a total nightmare," John said, smiling.

"Let's do it," Jessie decided. "Either way it'll be interesting."

Chapter Twenty-Four

"I cannot believe we're doing this," Jessie said as she, Emma and Natalie got out of the taxi in Times Square.

"*You* can't believe it?!" Emma laughed. "At least they're your family. I'm along on what could well be the most awkward dinner of all time and I'm not even related."

Jessie laughed. "True. You don't have to join in, though. Think of it like watching a documentary."

Jessie, Emma, John and Rhys had spent the day doing the museums while Natalie had worked. They'd been to the Natural History Museum, the Guggenheim and MoMA. They'd wanted to go to The Met so Jessie could see The Temple of Dendur, which features in *When Harry Met Sally*, but it was closed on Mondays. They'd seen some amazing things, eaten great food (the museums had wonderful cafeterias) and taken full advantage of the air conditioning, since it was one of the hottest days so far.

In fact, it was still extremely warm, even at 8pm, so they waited for John and Rhys – who'd gone back to their hotel to change – in the shade of the building. Jessie looked around. Further down the road, Spongebob Squarepants – or rather someone dressed as Spongebob Squarepants – was having his photograph taken with tourists. In the opposite direction, the Naked Cowboy was doing the same.

"I'm really hungry," Emma said.

"Me too," Jessie said.

"There's Ben," Natalie said.

Jessie and Emma turned to look the way Natalie was looking. Ben was walking towards them, wearing jeans and a white shirt.

Jessie looked at her mum who was beaming at Ben. She looked at Ben. He looked a bit bashful –

presumably Natalie had told him what Jessie had seen – but he was grinning back at Natalie. As he joined them, another cab pulled up and John and Rhys got out.

Natalie made all the introductions and then they went inside. They had to get an express lift up to the restaurant, which was the only revolving restaurant in New York. They all rode in silence while their ears popped and their stomachs flipped.

Up on the 48th floor, Jessie and Emma followed Natalie and Ben and John and Rhys to their table by the window.

Natalie and Ben were holding hands and Emma nudged Jess. "Are you OK about this?" she whispered.

"Yeah. I think they're in love." She pulled a face.

"It's probably that sexual prime thing," Emma said. "Aren't teenage boys and women in their late thirties both at their peak?"

"Oh my God! Thanks for that!"

Emma laughed. "You're so repressed."

"You'll be sorry if she brings him back tonight and we have to listen to them at it."

"She wouldn't," Emma said. "Not with us there."

"You're probably right," Jessie said.

"She'll probably go back to his place," Emma said and Jessie laughed.

"Oh well then, that's OK."

They all sat down at the circular table, which, even though it was still light, was set with candles.

"So," Jessie's dad said. "This is nice."

They all laughed.

"I know it's awkward," he continued. "But it'll be good to get to know each other better. We're all going to be in each other's lives after all. Apart from you, Emma. You can make a run for it now, if you like." He smiled.

"Maybe after I've eaten," Emma joked.

They ordered drinks and sat chatting and looking out at the view. The restaurant was revolving – slowly enough that it wasn't disorientating – and it was amazing to see the view changing in front of their eyes.

"I still can't quite believe I'm here," Jessie said.

"Me neither," her mum said, smiling.

"What, me or you?" Jessie asked.

"Both."

"Remember when she used to pretend she lived in New York?" John asked Natalie.

Jessie covered her face with her hands. "Oh great!"

Natalie laughed. "Oh God, yes! Do you know, I'd forgotten about that!"

"How old would you have been?" John asked Jessie, who had picked up a menu and was hiding behind it.

"She was about 14, wasn't she?" Natalie asked.

"12," Jessie said. "I was 12!"

"What did she do?" Rhys asked.

"She spoke in an American accent," John said.

Emma snorted Coke out of her nose. "Owwwww! Oh God, I forgot about that." She pinched her nose closed. "God, that really hurt."

"She would only watch American TV and read American books," John said.

"She made us go to that American football game at Old Trafford, do you remember?" Natalie asked John.

"Oh yes! Miami Dolphins, wasn't it?"

"Versus the New York Giants," Jessie added, still pretending to study the menu.

"Sounds like you had a good imagination," Rhys said.

"Yes. She gets it from me," Natalie said.

Jessie looked at her mum over the top of the menu and smiled.

Once they'd ordered, Jessie and Emma got up to find the loos.

"It's going well, isn't it?" Emma said.

"Seems to be, yes," Jessie said.

"It's all very healthy," Emma pronounced.

"Oh yes. They'll be suggesting we go to family therapy next. And I'll make you come with us."

Emma snorted. "No chance."

The bathrooms were in the centre of the restaurant and, as they walked back out, Jessie was amazed to see Finn. He was sitting at a table with a man and woman who were presumably his parents. He was wearing a pink shirt and he looked gorgeous.

"Oh my God," Jessie whispered.

"I know," Emma said. "I've just seen him too. Stay calm."

They walked back to their table, both holding themselves slightly self-consciously and trying not to look back at Finn's table.

"What's wrong with you two?" John asked, when they sat down.

Jessie looked at Emma – her cheeks were pink and her eyes bright. She assumed she looked the same.

"We just saw someone we kind of know," Jessie said.

"Here?" her mum asked. "Who?"

"A boy we met last night," Emma said.

"We should have known it was a boy," John muttered.

"Oh, I've been meaning to ask you," Natalie said. "What happened with...was it Tyler?"

"Taylor," Emma said instantly.

Jessie turned and Emma mouthed, "Sorry."

"Yeah, I went out with him a few times, but there's nothing going on now," Jessie said.

"So he's not waiting for you back in Manchester, pining away?" Rhys asked, smiling.

"Hell, no," Jessie said.

"Who's this boy then?" Natalie asked. "Where did you meet him?"

"We kind of gatecrashed his birthday party," Emma said.

"He said he loves your play," Jessie told her mum. "He said his mum's a theatre critic and she made him see it and he loved it."

Natalie, who had been looking rather suspicious at the idea of this random boy, suddenly beamed. "Really? I wonder who..."

She was interrupted by the arrival of the starters. Conversation stopped while they all tucked in.

Chapter Twenty-Five

Finn's parents had sprung dinner at The View on him when he and his dad had got home from work. They'd had one of their first dates there so it had always been their favourite 'special occasion' restaurant. He liked it too – you never did get tired of the view. Although this time they'd been seated away from the windows, which was disappointing.

They'd just ordered when Finn saw Jessie and Emma coming out of the bathrooms. At first he'd thought he was hallucinating, particularly since he'd just that minute been thinking about Jessie.

Since seeing Scott his internal monologue had switched from 'What am I going to do about Sam?'

to 'Will I see Jessie again?' And then he worried that he was just replacing his Sam obsession with a new, different obsession. Particularly since Jessie was only in New York for the summer. Was he only ever going to be interested in unattainable girls? Was it his way of protecting himself or something? Although if that was the case, it wasn't working.

He felt so relieved that Sam was leaving. Which made him feel guilty about Scott, who was obviously upset. But he almost felt like he'd been freed from his obsession. In fact, it was even more than that. He felt like he'd been hypnotised and someone had clapped and woken him up. And not just about Sam. He kept thinking about what Jessie had said. About how her mom thought everything in terms of how it related to her instead of realising Jessie was a person in her own right.

He looked at his parents who were both studying the menu, even though they each had the same thing every time they came: his dad the steak and his mom the salmon.

"Mom. Dad," he said. "I need to talk to you about something."

His mom took off her glasses and placed them on the table in front of her. His dad smiled distractedly.

"I'm just going to come right out and say it," Finn said.

He saw something like alarm flash across his dad's face and he wondered if he thought he was going to tell them he was gay. He almost smiled.

"I'm changing my major," he said.

"No," his dad said. "You're not."

Finn took a breath. "Sorry. What I meant to say was that I'd very much like to change my major and I would be appreciate your support."

"No," his dad said again.

"What is it you want to change to?" his mom asked, frowning.

"Architecture. I—"

His dad interrupted with a snort, but his mum held her hand up to him, to indicate he should let Finn finish.

"I've looked into it. I've read the prospectus. I can do a minor in business."

"Since when were you interested in architecture?" his dad asked and Finn almost laughed.

"I've always been interested. I've been obsessed with the Empire State Building for years, haven't I? Isn't that why I'm working there with you?"

"No. You're working there to learn about business."

"But I'm not interested in business. And I don't want to study business!"

"We all have to do things we don't want to do," his dad said.

"But why do we?" Finn asked.

"That's life. That's being an adult."

"Maybe it is for you, but I don't want that to be what it's like for me. And this isn't about you. It isn't about Gran. It's about me. My future. Are you seriously saying that I can't choose it for myself? Are you seriously saying you're going to make that choice for me? That you know better?"

"No," Diane said. "He's not saying that. Are you? Charles?"

Finn's dad took his glasses off and rubbed

his face. "No. No, I'm not saying that. We can... discuss it."

"Yeah?" Finn asked.

"Yes," his father replied.

Grinning, Finn picked up his menu.

Chapter Twenty-Six

Once they'd all finished their main meals, Jessie stood up, planning to head back to the bathroom.

"You off to the loo again?" her dad asked and Jessie gave him a hard stare.

"Oh yes, there's a boy, isn't there," he said, grinning. "Sorry, I forgot."

Emma went too and they tried to casually look for Finn on the way, but they couldn't see him.

"Maybe they've already left," Emma said.

"Do you think so?" Jessie asked. "I should've had a look at what they were eating. Maybe they were on desserts."

"Yeah, that would've been nice and casual

– you peering over, checking out what was on their plates."

They went in the bathroom and fixed their hair and make-up. Jessie borrowed Emma's mascara and added another coat to her eyes.

"I've always wondered why you do that face when you put mascara on," Emma said, smiling.

"What face?" Jessie asked, looking up to do her lower lashes.

"You hold your mouth in a really weird way." Emma did an impression and Jessie laughed, "I don't do that!"

"You do," Emma said. "And your mum does it too."

"Does she?" Jessie asked.

Emma nodded.

"That's weird."

"Not really. Did she ever show you how to use make-up?"

"Not that I remember."

"Maybe you just learned from watching her."

"I must've done," Jessie said. She handed the mascara back to Emma.

"You might want to do the other eye," Emma said, grinning.

Once they'd finished, they headed back to the restaurant, stopping again to – casually – look for Finn.

"He's not here," Jessie said, after scanning all the nearby tables.

"Doesn't look like it, no," Emma agreed.

"Crap."

"If you really like him, we could find out which apartment he's in, you know."

"And do what? Knock on his door and ask him if he wants to come out and play?"

"Something like that, yes! Why not?"

"Why not?!" Jessie said. She looked so incredulous that Emma laughed.

They looked around again, but still nothing.

"Well, that's disappointing," Jessie said.

"What's disappointing?" Finn asked from behind them.

"Argh!" Emma said and then burst out laughing.

"What?" Finn asked, grinning.

"We were just—" Jessie started. Her cheeks were bright red.

"We were looking for you," Emma interrupted. "We saw you earlier when we came out of the bathroom, but then...ohhhhh!" She said, realising, and started to laugh.

"What?" Jessie asked.

Emma and Finn grinned at her.

"WHAT?"

"The bathrooms don't revolve," Finn said, smiling. "The rest of the restaurant revolves around them."

"Ohhhhh," Jessie said. She put her hands to her hot cheeks. "Well that's not at all embarrassing."

Finn grinned. "It's really nice to see you."

"You too," Jessie said, her hands still on her cheeks.

"You're not here on your own...?"

"No," Jessie said. "Far from it. We're with my parents. And their boyfriends."

Finn's eyebrows shot up. "Really? How is it? Sounds awkward?"

"Do you know, it's really not," Jessie said. "We're all talking and it's...you know, it's definitely weird, yeah. But it's OK."

"To be fair," Emma said. "Ben hasn't said a word yet. If he ever opens his mouth all hell might break loose."

They smiled.

"I think he's the strong, silent type," Jessie said. "And he's probably terrified. What about you, who are you with?" she asked Finn.

"My parents. Another birthday celebration. Or at least it was, until I told them I want to change my major."

"Ooh," Jessie said. "How did they take it?"

"Not as bad as I thought. They're not happy, mainly my dad. But I think they'll be OK. I have to thank you actually."

"Me?" Jessie asked.

"Yeah. It was talking to you last night that made me realise I had to tell them."

"Well. OK," Jessie said. "I don't know what I said, but I'm glad it helped."

They smiled at each other and then Emma cleared

her throat, dramatically, and they both looked at her.

"We should swap numbers," Finn said.

Once Finn had gone back to his parents, Jessie and Emma headed back to their table. As they approached, they saw that John and Rhys weren't there and Natalie and Ben were looking very cosy.

"Oh God," Jessie said. "Are they kissing?"

Emma nodded. Jessie put one hand up to shield her eyes.

"I think it's sweet," Emma said. "My mum and dad never kiss."

"Ben is not my dad!" Jessie said, outraged.

Emma burst out laughing, causing Natalie and Ben to spring apart, guiltily.

"Yeah, I should think so," Jessie grumbled.

"Sorry," Natalie said, beaming. She didn't look sorry.

Jessie blinked. She realised that even as recently as yesterday she would have assumed Natalie had been kissing Ben to embarrass her or to rub her face in her happiness or even to make Jessie envious that her mum had Ben and she didn't. Today she realised that it was simply that her mum was kissing her boyfriend. It had nothing to do with her. She found herself beaming back.

"Where're Dad and Rhys?" Jessie asked. She really hoped they hadn't gone off somewhere for a snog too.

"Your dad had a phone call so he went through to the bar, I think. And Rhys is in the bathroom. Didn't you see him?"

"No," Emma said. "Turns out the bathrooms are a lot more complicated than we ever imagined."

"How can a bathroom be complicated?" Ben asked. It was the only thing he said all evening.

Chapter Twenty-Seven

Jessie and Emma spent most of the following day showing John and Rhys around New York. Or rather, following John and Rhys around New York. They'd both been there loads of times and wanted to share a few of their favourite haunts.

For lunch, they went to Chinatown, where the air seemed even hotter and thicker than in the rest of the city and smelled of ginger and garlic and lemon. Lights and bunting were strung across the tightly-packed streets and brightly coloured flags and signs hung outside every building, along with the metal fire escapes that criss-crossed each one. They ate delicious dim sum in a restaurant with bright red skinned rabbits hanging upside down in the window, which would normally have put Jessie off, but she was way too hungry to care.

From there, they wandered over to the Strand Bookstore, where John and Rhys browsed until Jessie and Emma were begging them to leave and then – to the girls' horror – they headed straight for yet another bookshop.

After stopping for coffee they shopped in Soho and Jessie and Emma got their own back by spending even longer in Anthropologie than John and Rhys had spent in the bookshops. John eventually bought them something (a bag for Emma and a pair of shoes for Jessie) to get them to leave.

They decided to head back up to the apartment, but while they waited for a taxi, Jessie said, "Why don't we go to the Empire State Building?"

"What? Now?" John asked.

"Yes!" she said. "It's such a gorgeous day. It's so clear and it's not too hot…"

"Not too hot?!" Rhys said, incredulously. He'd been complaining about the heat all day.

"I know it's hard to believe," Jessie said, "but it's nowhere near as hot today as it has been. It's a lovely day! Come on!"

The others laughed.

"I don't know how you've still got the strength," John said. "I'm knackered."

"I'm just worried we're never going to go," Jessie said. "I've been trying to convince Em, but she's scared of heights. I don't want to miss it."

"Oh don't worry," Rhys said. "I'm sure you'll get your chance."

"Today!" Jessie said. "I want to go today. Who's with me?"

They all just blinked at her.

"Oh for goodness sake!" Jessie said. "Seriously? You won't come?"

"You know I don't like heights," Emma said.

"You were fine on that roof terrace!" Jessie said.

"I was not fine. I was distracted by you and Finn making gooey eyes at each other, but—"

"You and Finn were making gooey eyes?" Jessie's dad – who'd given up all attempts to flag down a cab – asked. "Who's Finn again?"

"We met him at the party," Jessie said. "And we weren't making 'gooey eyes'."

"And he's the one you saw at the restaurant last night too?" John asked.

"Yes," Jessie said.

"Did you arrange to meet him there?"

"No. He was there with his parents. And we didn't even know we were going there, if you remember."

"Is he stalking you?"

Jessie laughed. "No! We just keep...bumping into him. He lives in mum's building."

"Hang on," John said. "I'm not getting this. He lives in your mum's building? But you met him at a party downtown?"

Jessie nodded.

"Were you invited to the party?"

"No. We just went there after I, you know, freaked out and ran out of the theatre."

"But you knew about the party?"

"Could we go somewhere with air conditioning to have this conversation?" Rhys asked.

"The Empire State Building's probably air-conditioned," Jessie said.

"We're not going to the Empire State Building!" Emma said.

"Can we go tomorrow then?" Jessie asked.

"I've got a meeting tomorrow," John said and then asked Jessie again: "So you knew about the party?"

"No," Jessie said. "We asked the cab driver to recommend a hotel and it happened to be Finn's party."

"That's a bit of a coincidence, isn't it?" John said.

"It is a bit," Jessie said. "Yes. But so what?"

"And then he was at the restaurant last night?"

"Yes!"

John threw his arms up in exasperation. "And you don't think that's odd?"

"I do," Jessie said. "I do think that's odd, yes. But so what? Strange things happen! Maybe it's fate!"

John and Rhys both laughed.

"What?!" Jessie said.

"I don't believe in fate," John said.

"You don't have to," Jessie said. "You're not the one who keeps bumping into Finn."

John stared at her for a moment and then burst out laughing. "Right. OK. I keep forgetting that you're growing up." He pulled her towards him for a hug. "If you think he's OK then I'll trust your judgement."

"Thank you!" Jess said, laughing. "And if anyone mentions Taylor I'll punch them," she added. "So are we getting a cab to the Empire State or what?"

"You can," John said. "But I think you'll have to go on your own."

"Fine," Jessie said. "I'll go on my own. You lot would only spoil it anyway." She grinned.

John finally managed to flag down a cab and Jessie climbed in.

"Be careful," he said, before shutting the door and blowing her a kiss.

As the cab pulled out into the traffic, Jessie turned and looked back through the window. Her dad was trying to wave down another cab, but Emma and Rhys were heading over to a bench for a sit down. Jessie laughed and turned around to face the front again.

She was on her way to the Empire State Building. Finally.

***

Chapter Twenty-Eight

Finn couldn't concentrate on the job. Partly because it was so mind-numbingly boring, but mainly because he couldn't stop thinking about Columbia. And Jessie. In fact, Columbia and Jessie had become linked in his head. He couldn't believe it when he'd seen her the night before, just when he'd broached the subject of changing his major with his parents. It was like she was his guardian angel or something.

He leaned forward slowly and banged his head on his desk. Guardian angel? He was losing it.

Sitting back up, he looked again at the paperwork on his desk. Another list of insurance claims to input. How his dad thought data entry was going to teach him about business, he wasn't sure. Maybe what his dad wanted him to learn was the soul-sucking tedium of a cubicle job. If that was the case, then it had been a huge success.

He typed in one more claim and then checked the clock: 1.30. He'd arranged to meet Scott at 2 at the deli he worked in. It was only about 15 minutes' walk away, but, whatever. He'd walk slowly. He put the list of claims in his desk drawer and locked it, before also locking his computer. Writing 'Gone to lunch' on a post-it, he left.

He headed down 5th Avenue as far as Madison Square Park. It was another hot day, but not as humid as it had been and so he didn't feel too bad walking – even in his suit. At the other side of the park, he realised he was exactly where he'd overheard Jessie talking about the Empire State Building and decided it was a sign. He smiled. He'd thought he'd lost it then. Now he'd been thinking she was his friggin' guardian angel.

But it was weird how he kept bumping into her. It was definitely enough to make him believe in fate. At the very least, it reinforced the idea in Jessie's mom's play – that all of your decisions, even the smallest, had consequences. Even last night – if he hadn't gone to the bathroom when he did, he might not have seen Jessie and Emma again. Weird to think something really important could be affected by whether or not you needed to take a leak.

He walked down Broadway to Union Square, through the farmers' market and on towards the Strand. As he approached, he thought he saw Jessie and Emma going in, but shook his head to clear it. He obviously had low blood sugar or something. He knew he should have had a bigger breakfast.

He got to Scott's deli about fifteen minutes early and loitered, considering going back to the Strand, but then Scott spotted him through the window and waved him in. Finn went up to the counter.

"I won't be long. What do you want to eat?"

Finn looked up at the menu board above the counter.

"The sesame fried chicken is really good," Scott said.

"Great," Finn said.

"You want a coffee? Or a Coke?"

"I'll have a Coke," Finn said. "Thanks."

He sat at the bar at the window, looking out at Broadway. There was a fire truck parked opposite and he squinted to read the names painted on the door of the Engine 54 firefighters who died on 9/11.

Scott brought Finn's Coke – and a coffee for himself – and sat down.

"So what's up?" he asked.

Finn told him about work. It didn't take long. And then he told him about his parents' reaction to the idea of him changing his major.

Scott whistled through his teeth. "Have they said anything since?"

Finn shook his head. "I think they're going to be OK with it, you know? I think Dad was actually impressed that I'd done so much research. That I know what I'm talking about. It'll take a while for him to let go of what he wants me to do, I'm sure, but I think Mom'll come around faster."

They both looked out onto the street as the fire truck pulled away.

"Someone told me part of the reason crime came

down in the city is this kind of window seating," Scott said. "You know, 'cos people are obviously less likely to commit a crime if they think someone might be watching."

"Yeah?"

"Yeah. I don't know if it's true, but I like the idea. Good to think just sitting and having a coffee could make a difference."

Finn smiled. "I was just thinking about that kind of thing on the way here."

"What?" Scott asked.

"You know...fate and random events. That kind of thing."

Scott smiled. "You're going all philosophical are you? Is the air too thin at the ESB?"

"Nah. It's just...I've met a girl."

Scott's eyebrows shot up. "Really? Tell me more."

"She's – her name's Jessie – she's English and she's just here for the summer—"

Scott pulled a face. "You've fallen for a tourist?"

"She's not really a tourist. Her mom lives here, she's visiting her. And I haven't 'fallen for her', I haven't even taken her out."

"So...what? You've seen her through a window? What?"

"We just keep bumping into each other. And I like her. I think she likes me. That's what I was thinking about. How, you know, in a city this size..."

"That happens though. Eight million people and I bumped into Sam yesterday."

Finn felt his stomach clench at the sound of her name. But it didn't feel good the way it had in the past, this felt more like guilt at kissing her. Here he was with Scott, his best friend, who had no idea he'd kissed his girlfriend.

"Where?" Finn asked.

"Bagel place near Washington Square."

"Did you talk?"

"Yeah. A bit. She leaves next week. She apologised for the way she told me. It's cool."

"Is it? You OK?"

"Yeah. I mean...I really liked her, you know? But she's leaving. And that's it. Oh and she said to tell you goodbye too."

Finn winced. He felt like he wasn't breathing

properly. Like he was huffing for breath. He gulped his Coke.

"I liked her," Finn blurted.

"I know you did, man. Everyone did."

"No. I mean, I *like* liked her. I was crazy about her."

Scott stared at him, his expression unreadable. After a few seconds during which Finn felt sweat pooling at the base of his back, Scott said, "Seriously?"

Finn almost laughed. "Yes. Seriously. I couldn't stop thinking about her."

"When?"

"All the time."

Scott laughed then. "No, I mean when did it start?"

Finn felt relieved. If he was laughing, it was going to be OK, right? " Pretty much as soon as I met her," he said. "I couldn't believe how lucky you were to have met her first."

Scott rubbed his face with the flat of his hand. "Wow."

"I know."

"But you didn't...you didn't do anything?"

Finn swallowed. "I kissed her. At my party. I don't know what I was thinking."

Scott shook his head. "You kissed her?"

"Yeah. You'd gone and I'd had a couple of drinks and I bumped into her and...I think I lost my mind. There's no excuse. I just kissed her. And she smashed her glass and yelled at me and left and... I'm a dick. I know."

Scott was staring out at the street. "You really liked her?"

"Yeah."

"That's why you went to the airport that time?"

Finn realised his leg was jiggling and tried to make it stop. "Yes."

"Huh," Scott said.

Finn gulped more Coke. He couldn't tell what Scott was thinking, but he hadn't hit him so that had to be positive. "I'm really sorry, man," he said eventually.

"No, it's OK. I mean, she was gorgeous. I can't blame you for liking her. I just...I didn't think the two of you had much in common."

"No, I know. We didn't. It wasn't even real. Once I kissed her it all kind of went away."

Scott laughed. "You really need a girlfriend, man."

Finn laughed too. "Don't I know it."

When Finn got back to his desk, there was a second note under his 'Gone to lunch' post-it note. It said 'Pls see Charles asap.' Finn walked round to his office. Unlike Finn's cubicle, his dad's office had windows offering an incredible view of midtown. Finn stared out of the window for a second, before sitting down and smiling at his dad.

"Good lunch?" Charles asked.

Finn automatically looked at the clock and then mentally kicked him himself. Yes, he'd had longer than an hour for lunch, but was it really that big a deal? That was exactly the kind of thing he'd already come to hate about working in an office.

"Yeah, thanks. I met Scott."

"How is he?"

"Good, yeah."

"OK. So." Charles leaned forward and steepled his fingers under his chin. Finn knew this was his dad's 'serious conversation' position. Finn's leg started to jiggle.

"Changing your major."

"Yes," Finn said.

"Your mom and I are happy for you to do that."

Finn grinned and started to stand, but his dad held up one hand and he sat back down.

"There are conditions."

"Of course," Finn said.

"I want you to do a business course."

"OK."

"And I want you to continue to work here in the holidays unless you find an architecture-related internship."

"That's fine."

"I just want you to know that I'm not convinced by this, but you're 18 and I realise I need to trust that you know what you want to do."

"I appreciate that," Finn said.

Charles rolled his shoulders back and coughed. "If your grandmother had done the same then I probably wouldn't be here."

Finn felt his eyebrows shoot up. He'd never heard

his dad admit to anything like that before. "Where would you be?" he asked.

Charles smiled. "Oh, I don't know. I didn't know what I wanted to do, which is partly why I just went along with what my parents wanted me to do. But... no one grows up wanting to work in insurance, do they?"

Finn laughed. "Probably not, no. Cool office though."

"Very cool," his dad said.

At 6pm, Finn shut down his computer and left the office. His afternoon had been considerably better than his morning. Now that he knew he wasn't going to be stuck there forever – that he was actually going to get to do the thing he really wanted to do – he thought he could cope with his summer job much better.

Chapter Twenty-Nine

Jessie could hardly wait to get to the Empire State Building. All the way there, she stared out of the window. New York. She wasn't entirely sure what it was about the place that she loved so much, but she felt energised. New York was just so much *more* than Manchester. It was as if she'd been living in black and white and now everything was in colour with the volume turned right up.

Jessie realised she'd been staring at a branch of Bank of America for quite some time.

She leaned forward and slid the Perspex across. "How far away are we?" she asked the driver.

"Just round the corner," he said. "Ya wanna get out?"

Jessie paid him, got out of the cab and looked around. She knew she just needed to walk to the end of the street to work out exactly where she was. She set off in the direction of traffic. After almost bumping into a group of tourists, she stopped and asked one of them, "Do you know where the Empire State Building is?"

They all laughed. "Look up!" said one.

Jessie looked up at her favourite building. When she looked back down, Finn was standing in front of her, grinning.

"Hey," he said.

Jessie grinned back at him, "Hi."

"Should we even bother to discuss how weird it is bumping into each other again?" he said.

Jessie laughed. "I don't think so. You're not following me, are you?"

"Nope. Are you following me?"

Jessie shook her head, smiling.

"Are you going up or have you been up?" Finn gestured at the skyscraper they were standing under.

"Going up," Jessie said.

"On your own?"

"Yeah. Everyone else was either too busy, too tired or too scared of heights."

"Right," Finn said.

They smiled at each other and then Finn said, "I could come up with you. You know, if ...you wouldn't mind. And it would be faster because I've got a pass, you know, from working here? I don't have to—"

"That would be great," Jessie said.

They walked around onto Fifth Avenue, bypassed the queues and Finn showed his pass to the security guard. Once they were inside, Jessie looked around, astonished. The foyer was beautiful, despite being crammed with people. She recognised it instantly from lots of films, particularly *Sleepless in Seattle*. Finn showed his pass again and they were shown to a lift.

"I actually feel nervous," Jessie said, once the doors had closed and they'd started to move.

"About the height?" Finn asked.

"No, not really. More about finally going up there. It's been something I've wanted to do for so long."

"I get that," Finn said. "But you won't be disappointed, I know."

The lift seemed both faster and slower than Jessie had expected. The numbers were skipping past, but there were just so many of them. Finally they arrived at the 102nd floor. They stepped out of the lift, into a gift shop. Finn guided Jessie through the shop and then they stepped out onto the Observation Deck.

And Jessie started to cry.

"Oh God, I'm sorry," she said, wiping her face with her hands. "So embarrassing."

Finn smiled, "It's not. Don't worry."

They walked around a little until they could find a space and then stepped up to look out over Manhattan.

"Wow," Jessie breathed.

Jessie stared out over the buildings to the water beyond.

"Do you get used to this?" she asked Finn. "Living here?"

"No," Finn said. "Not really. You do forget sometimes, but then you'll see the sun shining on the Chrysler Building or...there's this really weird thing – when you're downtown and the sun's in a certain position, if you look back uptown the Empire State looks like a pencil drawing, you can't see any colour in it at all. I thought I was hallucinating the first time I saw it."

"I've seen it," Jessie said. "It was that day you overheard me and Emma talking about my dad, I think."

Finn laughed. "It really is weird, isn't it? The way we keep bumping into each other?" Finn said.

Jessie nodded. "It is, but at the same time it doesn't really feel weird. At least, it doesn't to me. My dad thinks it's a bit suspicious though."

Finn laughed. "I bet he does. I was talking to Scott about it at lunch and—"

"Is he OK?" Jessie interrupted. "What happened with Sam?"

"Oh God, yeah," Finn said. "She's moving to LA – where her dad is. And I told Scott – just today – I told him I kissed her."

"Wow," Jessie said. "What did he say?"

"He was OK about it. He—"

A couple of people were trying to squeeze in next to Jessie and Finn to look out at the view. Finn rolled his eyes at Jessie and they stepped out of the way and walked around the viewing deck until they found another space.

"So Scott wasn't angry?" Jessie asked.

"No. I think he was confused more than anything. He didn't think Sam was my type."

Jessie laughed. "That sounds very understanding of him!"

"Yeah well we've been friends a long time. And he's had a lot of girlfriends. And he was right. I was always so mad that Scott had met Sam first, you know? That if I'd met her first, it would have been me. But it wouldn't have been, because we didn't really have anything in common. When I think about it now, it was as if I had an imaginary Sam alongside the real Sam."

"That's what it was like for me with my ex, Taylor," Jessie said. "I had an idea of the boyfriend I wanted and I tried to make it him. But he really wasn't right. At least he was real though. My first boyfriend was totally imaginary. Actually, it was even more embarrassing than that..." Jessie couldn't believe she was going to admit this.

"Yeah?" Finn asked.

"Yeah. You remember *Sesame Street*? It was Super Grover."

"You're kidding?" Finn said.

Jessie laughed. "No. Shameful, isn't it?"

Finn laughed then. "No. Not at all."

They smiled at each other. Jessie noticed Finn glance down at her lips, but then he was looking in her eyes. Jessie suddenly felt like she couldn't breathe. Like she'd literally forgotten how. She stared back at him.

But then they weren't staring anymore. Suddenly – and Jessie didn't quite know how it had happened – suddenly they were kissing. Finn's lips were soft and warm. Jessie opened her eyes long enough to see that Finn's eyes were closed and closed hers again.

She felt his hand on her neck; his thumb stroked her jaw. Jessie was aware of a strange feeling in her knees. It felt like her bones were liquefying. Finn leaned back against the wall and Jessie leaned against him. He smelled gorgeous. Warm and salty and lemony.

And then they weren't kissing anymore. They smiled at each other.

"I feel like I've known you for..." Finn started.

"I know," Jessie said. "Me too."

"And we definitely haven't met before?"

"I don't think so," Jessie said. She looked down at Finn's mouth – there was a freckle on his jaw she hadn't noticed before – and then up into his eyes again. "Have you ever been to Manchester?"

"No," Finn said. He slid his hand down Jessie's arm and held her hand. "Have you been to New York before?"

Jessie shook her head.

"I guess it's a mystery then," Finn said.

"It is," Jessie said.

Finn wrapped his arms around her again. Jessie rested her head on his chest for a moment and then she looked up, over his shoulder, at New York. She tried to memorise every single detail so she could think back on this moment – this perfect moment – for the rest of her life.

Epilogue

Sitting in Verdi Square, Jessie finished the juice she'd bought from Gray's Papaya and checked the time on her phone: 8am.

Jessie loved the mornings because they were that tiny bit cooler and everything seemed somehow sharper. People were heading off to work and there was an air of expectation. It made Jessie think of that expression: 'Today is the first day of the rest of your life'. She'd first seen it on a poster years ago and she'd made her parents laugh by trying to get them to explain it. Of course today was the first day of the rest of your life, she'd thought at the time. What else could it be? But in New York she understood. The rest of your life didn't have to be the same as the life you'd had before. Today could be the first day of a new life.

"Hey," Finn said, lifting up her ponytail and kissing her on the back of the neck. "We'll have to stop meeting like this."

"Good morning," Jessie smiled.

He sat down on the bench next to her and kissed her properly.

"Did Emma get away OK?" he asked, a few minutes later.

"Yeah." She handed him the breakfast bagel she'd bought him.

"Thanks." He kissed her again. "Did she cry?"

Jessie nodded.

"Did you?"

Jessie nodded again.

"But you'll be back there in a couple of weeks!" Finn said, unwrapping his breakfast.

"I know," Jessie said. "But not for long. It just seemed really...final. Like she was leaving me here."

Finn squeezed her hand. "What are you going to be like leaving Manchester then?"

"I don't know," Jessie said. "But I'll be OK when I get back here."

"I should think so," Finn smiled.

"I still can't believe I'm going to be living here," Jessie said.

"Me neither. When does your dad's office open?"

"Not until next year. Don't worry, it'll be open in time for your internship."

"Excellent. And you're going to meet me here and buy me breakfast every day, yeah?"

Jessie smiled. "You'll be lucky."

"I feel lucky," Finn said and smiled back.

THE END

Acknowledgements

A HUGE thank you to...

My agent, Alice, and editor, Catherine, for being lovely, encouraging and tolerant of my telephone waffling and diva tendencies.

Mike Lemanski and Thy Bui for the gorgeous cover that made me cry.

Emma Davies, Helen Jackson, Jenni Nock, Louise Jones and Michelle Cardozo for reading an early draft and giving fabulous feedback.

The friends I've shared New York with: David, Leanne, Lisa Clark, Jo and Andy, Diane and Maz.

Susan Robinson, Sarah Goldsack, Diane Shipley, Erin Hitzke, Luisa Plaja and Stella McLoughlin for keeping me sane.

Twitter. I couldn't have done it without you. Seriously.

The We Should Be Writing women for being my first and best writing buddies.

New writing comrades Cat, Fiona, Gillian, Keren, Kay, Luisa, Sophia, Susie and Tamsyn for being supportive, fabulous and hilarious.

Everyone who loved Della Says: OMG! and took the time to tell me so.

Finally, the biggest thank you of all to David, Harry and Joe for being the family of my dreams. Love you.

Win a trip to New York City!

Do you fancy following in the footsteps of Jessie
and Emma and taking a trip to New York?
Want to hunt down all the *Sex and the City* locations,
stroll around Central Park, check out a play on Broadway,
and find your very own Finn?!

Here's your chance!

Orchard Books are offering one lucky reader
a trip to the Big Apple with a friend or chaperone.
We'll pay for your flights, a three-night
stay and money to cover all your meals.

All you have to do is visit
www.jessieheartsnyc.com to enter.

Good luck!

Competition closes on 31st October 2011. Open to UK and ROI residents only.
Terms and conditions apply.
Please see www.jessieheartsnyc.com for more details.

ORCHARD BOOKS
www.orchardbooks.co.uk
www.keris-stainton.com

Keris Stainton's
New York Top Fives!

Top five books set in New York

The Princess Diaries by Meg Cabot
Meg Cabot is my favourite YA author and I love her *Princess Diaries* series so much that if I ever have a daughter I plan to name her Mia.

Eloise by Kay Thompson
Eloise lives in New York's Plaza Hotel along with her pug Weenie and her turtle Skipperdee. She's awesome, obv.

From the Mixed up Files of Mrs Basil E Frankweiler by E L Konigsburg
11-year-old Claudia and her younger brother Jamie run away to New York's Metropolitan Museum of Art. *Eloise* made me want to live in a hotel and this book made me want to live in a museum.

A Cricket in Times Square by George Selden
I read this as a child and I suspect it's where my New York obsession began.

Suite Scarlett by Maureen Johnson
And now we're back in a hotel! Scarlett Martin lives with her family in the falling-down Hopewell Hotel on the Upper East Side and it sounds wonderful.

Top five films set in New York

When Harry Met Sally
My favourite film of all time and a huge part of my New York obsession.

Nick & Norah's Infinite Playlist
New York + Michael Cera + Kat Dennings = LOVE

You've Got Mail
I would love this film for the animated titles alone. (I do wish Meg Ryan's character had been able to keep her bookshop though.)

Remember Me
This film blew me away. It also taught me (finally) to appreciate RPattz.

Mad Hot Ballroom
It's a documentary about underprivileged New York children learning ballroom dancing. And it's wonderful.

Top five New York places

Top of the Rock

The one failing of the Empire State Building is that you can't see the Empire State Building from there. You can see it from Top of the Rock though.

Strand Bookstore

18 miles of books. I think that's all you need to know.

Roosevelt Island Tram

It takes just a few minutes and only costs a couple of dollars, but the Roosevelt Island Tram (more like a cable car than a tram) gives you the most spectacular views of Manhattan. Also, as it sets off, you can see right into people's apartments. Excellent if you're nosy.

Central Park Zoo

It seems kind of funny to have a zoo right in the middle of a city, but once you're inside you forget you're even in New York.

TV & Movie Tour

I've done this tour quite a few times and, because so many movies are made in New York, it's been different each time. And it's always completely brilliant.

Top five songs about New York

New York by Paloma Faith

Give My Regards to Broadway by Barry Manilow

New York City by They Might Be Giants

Empire State of Mind (Part II) by Alicia Keys

New York Minute by Don Henley

Gallagher Academy
might claim to be a school
for geniuses – but it's really
a school for spies.

Cammie Morgan is fluent in fourteen languages
and capable of killing a man in seven different ways
(three of which involve a piece of uncooked spaghetti).

But she's only just beginning her most dangerous
mission yet – falling in love…

Don't miss all four books in Ally Carter's
***Gallagher Girls* series**

40830 951 3 £5.99 PB   978 1 40830 952 0 £5.99 PB   978 1 40830 953 7 £5.99 PB   978 1 40830 954 4 £5.99 PB
40831 412 8 £5.99 eBook   978 1 40831 414 2 £5.99 eBook   978 1 40831 439 5 £5.99 eBook   978 1 40831 541 5 £5.99 eBook

www.gallagheracademy.co.uk
www.facebook.com/gallagheracademy
ORCHARD BOOKS

Read on for a taster of

I'd Tell You I
L♥VE
YOU,
But Then
I'd Have To
KILL
YOU

Chapter 1

I suppose a lot of teenage girls feel invisible sometimes, like they just disappear. Well, that's me – Cammie the Chameleon. But I'm luckier than most because, at my school, that's considered cool.

I go to a school for spies.

Of course, technically, the Gallagher Academy for Exceptional Young Women is a school for *geniuses* – not *spies* – and we're free to pursue any career that befits our exceptional educations. But when a school tells you that, and then teaches you things like advanced encryption and fourteen different languages, it's kind of like big tobacco telling kids not to smoke; so all of us Gallagher Girls know lip service when we hear it. Even my mom rolls her eyes but doesn't correct me when I call it spy school, and *she's* the headmistress. Of course, she's also a retired CIA operative, and it was her idea for me to write this, my first Covert Operations Report, to summarise what happened last semester. She's always telling us that the worst part of the spy life isn't the danger – it's the paperwork. After all, when you're on a plane home from Istanbul with a nuclear warhead in a hatbox, the last thing you want to do is write a report about it. So that's why I'm writing this – for the practice.

If you've got a Level Four clearance or higher, you probably know all about us Gallagher Girls, since we've been around for more than a hundred years (the school, not me – I'll turn sixteen next month!). But if you don't have that kind of clearance, then you probably think we're just an urban spy myth – like jet packs and invisibility suits – and you drive by our ivy-covered walls, look at our gorgeous mansion and manicured grounds, and assume, like everyone else, that the Gallagher Academy for Exceptional Young Women is just a snooty boarding school for bored heiresses with no place else to go.

Well, to tell you the truth, we're totally fine with that – it's one of the reasons no one in the town of Roseville, Virginia, thought twice about the long line of limousines that brought my classmates back to school last September. I watched from a window seat on the third floor of the mansion as the cars materialised out of the blankets of green foliage and turned through the towering wrought-iron gates. The half-mile-long driveway curved through the hills, looking as harmless as Dorothy's yellow brick road, not giving a clue that it's equipped with laser beams that read tire treads and sensors that check for explosives, and one entire section that can open up and swallow a truck whole. (If you think that's dangerous, don't even get me started about the pond!)

I wrapped my arms around my knees and stared through the window's wavy glass. The red velvet curtains were drawn around the tiny alcove, and I was enveloped by an odd sense of peace, knowing that in twenty minutes, the corridors were going to be crowded; music was going to be blaring; and I was going to go from being an only child to one of a hundred sisters, so I knew to savour the silence while it lasted. Then, as if to prove my point, a loud blast and the smell of burning hair came floating up the main stairs from the second-floor Hall of History, followed by Professor Buckingham's distinguished voice crying, "Girls! I told you not to touch that!" The smell got worse, and one of the seventh graders was probably still on fire, because Professor Buckingham yelled, "Stand still. Stand still, I say!"

Then Professor Buckingham said some French swear words that the seventh graders probably wouldn't understand for three semesters, and I remembered how every year during new student orientation one of the newbies will get cocky and try to show off by grabbing the sword Gillian Gallagher used to slay the guy who was going to kill Abraham Lincoln–the first guy, that is. The one you never hear about.

But what the newbies aren't told on their tour of the school grounds is that Gilly's sword is charged with enough electricity to…well…light your hair on fire.

I just love the start of school.

I think our room used to be an attic, once upon a time. It has these cool alcoves and oddly shaped windows and lots of little nooks and crannies, where a girl can sit with her back against the wall and listen to the thundering feet and squeals of hello that are probably pretty standard at boarding schools everywhere on the first day after summer break (but they probably stop being standard when they take place in Portuguese and Farsi). Out in the hall, Kim Lee was talking about her summer in Singapore, and Tina Walters was declaring that "Cairo was super cool. Johannesburg – not so much", which is exactly what my mom had said when I'd complained about how Tina's parents were taking her to Africa over the summer whereas *I* was going to have to visit my dad's parents on their ranch in Nebraska; an experience I'm fairly sure will never help me break out of an enemy interrogation facility or disarm a dirty bomb.

"Hey, where's Cammie?" Tina asked, but I wasn't about to leave my room until I could come up with a story to match the international exploits of my classmates, seventy per cent of whom are the daughters of current or former government operatives – aka spies. Even Courtney Bauer had spent a week in Paris, and *her* parents are both optometrists, so you can see why I wasn't especially eager to admit that I'd spent three months plopped down right in the middle of North America, cleaning fish.

I'd finally decided to tell them about the time I was experimenting with average household items that can be used as weapons and accidentally decapitated a scarecrow (who knew knitting needles could do that kind of damage?), when I heard the distinctive thud of luggage crashing into a wall and a soft, Southern, "Oh, Cammie...come out, come out, wherever you are."

I peered around the corner and saw Liz posing in the doorway, trying to look like Miss Alabama, but bearing a greater resemblance to a toothpick in capri trousers and flip-flops. A very *red* toothpick.

She smiled and said, "Did you miss me?"

Well, I *did* miss her, but I was totally afraid to hug her. "What happened to you?"

Liz rolled her eyes and just said, "Don't fall asleep by a pool in Alabama," as if she should have known better – which she totally should have. I mean, we're all technically geniuses and everything, but at age nine, Liz had the highest score on the third grade achievement tests *ever*. The government keeps track of that kind of thing, so the summer before seventh grade, her parents got a visit from some big guys in dark suits and three months later, Liz was a Gallagher Girl – just not the kill-a-man-with-her-bare-hands variety. If I'm ever on a mission, I want Bex beside me and Liz far, far away, with about a dozen computers and a chessboard – a fact I couldn't help but remember when Liz tried to fling her suitcase onto the bed, but missed and ended up knocking over a bookcase, demolishing my stereo and flattening a perfectly-scaled replica of DNA that I'd made out of papier-mâché in eighth grade.

"Oopsy daisy," Liz said, throwing her hand to her mouth.

Sure, she knows swear words in fourteen different languages, but when faced with a minor catastrophe, Liz says *"oopsy daisy"*. At that point I didn't care how sunburned she was – I had to hug my friend.

At 6.30 exactly, we were in our uniforms, sliding our hands over the smooth mahogany banisters, and descending down the staircases that spiral gracefully to the foyer floor. Everyone was laughing (turns out my knitting needle story was a big hit), but Liz and I kept looking towards the door in the centre of the atrium below.

"Maybe there was trouble with the plane?" Liz whispered. "Or customs? Or…I'm sure she's just late."

I nodded and continued glancing down at the foyer as if, on cue, Bex was going to burst through the doors. But they stayed closed, and Liz's voice got squeakier as she asked, "Did you hear from her? I didn't hear from her. Why didn't we hear from her?"

Well, I would have been surprised if we *had* heard from her, to tell you the truth. As soon as Bex had told us that both her mom and her dad were taking a leave of absence to spend the summer with her, I knew she wasn't going to be much of a pen pal. Leave it to Liz to come to a completely different conclusion.

"Oh my gosh, what if she dropped out?" Liz cranked up the worry in her voice. "Did she get *kicked* out?"

"Why would you think that?"

"Well…" she said, stumbling over the obvious, "Bex always has been kind of *rules-optional.*" Liz shrugged, and, sadly, I couldn't disagree. "And why else would she be late? Gallagher Girls are never late! Cammie, you know something, don't you? You've got to know *something!*"

Times like this are when it's no fun being the headmistress's daughter, because A) it's totally annoying when people think I'm in a loop I'm not in, and B) people always assume I'm in partnership with the staff, which really I'm not. Sure, I have private dinners with my mom on Sunday nights, and *sometimes* she leaves me alone in her office for five seconds, but that's it. Whenever school is in session, I'm just another Gallagher Girl (except for being the girl to whom the aforementioned A and B apply).

One year + one beach house + zero parents =

978 1 408 30979 7 £6.99 Pbk Aug 2011

I was about to live a sixteen-year-old's dream.
House on the beach.
No parents.
Parties whenever we wanted.
Boys wherever we wanted.

April and her best friend, Vi, are living by themselves.
Of course, April's parents don't know that.
They think she's living with Vi and Vi's mum.
But it's not April's fault that her dad decided to move
away in the middle of high school.
So who could blame her for a little white lie?
Or the other nine things that April (probably) shouldn't
have done that year...

ORCHARD BOOKS
www.orchardbooks.co.uk